Andrew reached out for Miranda's hand.

"The last two weeks have been some of the best of my whole life. I'm sure that sounds stupid, but it's the truth."

She felt her heart flutter in the center of her chest. "It's not stupid. I feel the same way. I love having you here." She scanned his face and her knees went weak when he absentmindedly licked his lower lip.

Before she knew what was happening, she felt him lock his gaze on her.

His hand went to her jaw, his fingertips giving the lightest imaginable touch against her neck. "I'm afraid I'm going to make a mistake, Miranda."

"What do you mean?" She was desperate for the answer, but she also feared it. If he pulled away from her, she might never recover.

"I want to kiss you. But I worry that it's wrong."

She didn't know what to say. She was too relieved that they'd both been thinking the exact same thing. The only thing she cared about was hurrying down this path he'd just set them on.

"Maybe you should just try it and see how right it feels."

* * *

All He Wants for Christmas by Karen Booth is part of The Sterling Wives series.

Dear Reader,

It's time to wrap up The Sterling Wives trilogy with *All He Wants for Christmas*!

If you're jumping into the series, it started when a wealthy, enigmatic man died unexpectedly, leaving control of his company to his current wife, along with his two ex-wives. The three women are thrust into a partnership and, ultimately, a sisterhood.

All He Wants for Christmas is the final chapter, centered on Miranda, who has been widowed for a few months. She's also pregnant with her dead husband's baby! Miranda is clinging to all connections to her deceased husband, including his estranged brother, Andrew. The trouble is that virtually everyone sees Andrew as a bad actor. He spent years waging war with his brother. For Andrew, walking into Miranda's life isn't easy. He's fighting lies and secrets while trying to build a future. This is a love story between two people who desperately need each other. They just don't know it!

I hope you enjoy *All He Wants for Christmas*. Drop me a line anytime at karen@karenbooth.net. I love hearing from readers!

Karen

KAREN BOOTH

———

ALL HE WANTS FOR CHRISTMAS

HARLEQUIN®
DESIRE™

Recycling programs for this product may not exist in your area.

ISBN-13: 978-1-335-20948-1

All He Wants for Christmas

Copyright © 2020 by Karen Booth

All rights reserved. No part of this book may be used or reproduced in any manner whatsoever without written permission except in the case of brief quotations embodied in critical articles and reviews.

This is a work of fiction. Names, characters, places and incidents are either the product of the author's imagination or are used fictitiously. Any resemblance to actual persons, living or dead, businesses, companies, events or locales is entirely coincidental.

This edition published by arrangement with Harlequin Books S.A.

For questions and comments about the quality of this book, please contact us at CustomerService@Harlequin.com.

Harlequin Enterprises ULC
22 Adelaide St. West, 40th Floor
Toronto, Ontario M5H 4E3, Canada
www.Harlequin.com

Printed in U.S.A.

Karen Booth is a Midwestern girl transplanted in the South, raised on '80s music and repeated readings of *Forever* by Judy Blume. When she takes a break from the art of romance, she's listening to music with her college-aged kids or sweet-talking her husband into making her a cocktail. Learn more about Karen at karenbooth.net.

Books by Karen Booth

Harlequin Desire

The Sterling Wives

Once Forbidden, Twice Tempted
High Society Secrets
All He Wants for Christmas

The Eden Empire

A Christmas Temptation
A Cinderella Seduction
A Bet with Benefits
A Christmas Seduction
A Christmas Rendezvous

Visit her Author Profile page at Harlequin.com, or karenbooth.net, for more titles.

You can also find Karen Booth on Facebook, along with other Harlequin Desire authors, at Facebook.com/harlequindesireauthors!

For my aunt Judy,
who absolutely loved Christmas

One

Andrew Sterling had nearly forgotten how pleasant November in San Diego could be. As he descended the stairs of his Cessna, a soft breeze ruffled his hair and a strong dose of California sun warmed his face. If he had to guess, it was nearly seventy degrees today. This was a complete one-eighty from his adopted home of Seattle, where the cold and rain was a fixture this close to Thanksgiving. It crept into your bones and your psyche and made itself at home well past Christmas. San Diego was obviously a far better locale this time of year. But this city held too many unhappy memories for Andrew—dreams dashed, loyalties destroyed, love lost and, ultimately, two brothers forever divided. He wouldn't be staying here long, no matter how nice the weather.

Forever divided. That was the part Andrew was having the hardest time getting past. There was no repairing his relationship with his brother. Johnathon was dead, his life ended three short months ago at the too-young age of forty-one. It was a fluke accident—a line drive on the golf course, straight to the temple. There had been no time to say goodbye, not that it would have been an easy conversation. There would've been countless things to say, and even more things to apologize for, which could have only happened after getting past the state of their relationship that day—Johnathon and Andrew hadn't spoken in over a year. Even worse, Andrew was orchestrating a scheme to kneecap Johnathon's business, Sterling Enterprises.

He'd had good reason to embark on the secret venture, but that didn't matter now. Johnathon was gone, and Andrew had to stop the plan he'd set in motion. Defuse the bomb he'd built. Unfortunately, someone else still wanted to light the fuse—Andrew's onetime ally in the scheme, a man known only as Victor. Victor had been on the wrong end of a multimillion-dollar business deal with Johnathon and he was not the type to forgive and forget. Guilt and regret had made Andrew stop, but Victor didn't have family loyalty or even a conscience to constrain him. Victor was merciless. If he couldn't get his revenge on

Johnathon, he'd destroy his legacy instead. Hence, Andrew's open-ended return to the city he could no longer stand.

Andrew strode across the tarmac to the idling SUV waiting for him at Gray Municipal, a landing strip so far south of San Diego it was nearly in Mexico. No one would expect Andrew to come into town via such a remote and admittedly unglamorous location. There were more than a dozen airports closer to the city, with better amenities and far nicer facilities to hangar his plane. But he wanted to slip into San Diego undetected. It was the best way to stop Victor at his game.

It was a half-hour drive to the historic US Grant Hotel, the five-star grand dame of downtown San Diego, but Andrew was not delivered to the front door. Instead, he was taken to the parking garage and used the private entry reserved for dignitaries and heads of state. Andrew was neither, but he did have a security detail and the money that afforded this level of preferential treatment. He and one of his bodyguards, Pietro, rode the elevator up to the presidential suite. It was pure luxury, with its tall arched windows, nine-foot ceiling and impeccable decor, not that Andrew planned to enjoy it. Pietro did a quick sweep of the living area, then headed up to the suite's second level for a full inspection of the bedroom and bath. Meanwhile, Andrew paced. He was eager to get to work, discreetly find out exactly what Victor was up to, and formulate his plan from there.

"Everything checks out upstairs," Pietro said. "Would you like me to head over to check on Ms. Sterling?"

"Yes. Just please be discreet. She doesn't know yet what's going on." Andrew swallowed hard, thinking about Miranda, his brother's widow. She'd played a crucial role in Andrew's decision to stop the plan against Sterling Enterprises. Only she didn't know it.

Andrew had gone to see her two weeks after Johnathon's death, and that visit had been nothing like what he'd expected. She'd had every reason to be angry with him or send him away. Andrew had missed Johnathon's funeral, too shell-shocked to deal with the avalanche of emotions that came with his brother's sudden death. Instead, Miranda had been welcoming, inviting him into her showpiece of a home. Not that she let him off the hook completely. She told him flat out that his absence at the service had hurt. Andrew did his best to explain, but it was complicated. Then Miranda did what very few people had ever done—she forgave him.

Once the air was cleared, Miranda happily spent time with him, telling him about her life with Johnathon and, most important, about her baby on the way—the child his brother learned of on his death bed. Andrew dismissed the too-shiny version of his brother in the stories Miranda told. Johnathon had always created his own reality, twisting things until he could not be considered at fault. But Andrew did listen carefully when Miranda pondered her future, the one in which her child would never know its father. That part of the conversation had stuck to Andrew like glue. When it was time to go, she hugged him, kissed him on the cheek and referred to him as family. She'd placed her hand on her pregnant belly and told him that she hoped her baby would be part of his life. Even now, over two months later, the entire experience haunted him. He'd always known that family was important, but he'd never seen it. Or felt it. Not like that.

That made his decision for him. He immediately returned to Seattle and told Victor that the scheme to hurt Sterling Enterprises was over. Johnathon was gone and any revenge to be exacted was his. He'd come up with the plan to prevent Sterling Enterprises from winning the bid on a project for San Diego, the renovation of the Seaport Promenade, a large public space overlooking the bay. Andrew had chosen that project for very personal reasons, as he was certain Johnathon had done the same. It had been the site of a particularly painful chapter in the long rivalry between the two brothers—the day Andrew was left at the altar, or more precisely, the Seaport Promenade wedding pavilion.

"Please let me know if you see anything out of the ordinary," Andrew said to Pietro, forcing himself to shake off the unpleasant memories threatening to take hold.

"Of course, sir."

"I'd like you and the team to continue surveilling Victor's home here in San Diego, his usual haunts and the airports, as well. Please let me know if he bubbles to the surface."

"You'll be the first to know, Mr. Sterling."

Andrew saw Pietro to the door, closed the door behind him and latched it, then pulled out his phone to call a woman named Sandy. She'd played a key role in the plan as a mole placed inside Sterling Enterprises to help run the Seaport project aground. Sandy readily agreed to stop when Andrew asked her, but then Victor managed to lure her away with a great deal of money, and she went right back to work. Andrew had never pegged Sandy to be a person who cared only about money, but apparently she was.

Unfortunately, Andrew reached her voice mail. "Sandy. It's Andrew. Again. This is getting old. You won't answer your phone and neither will Victor. We need to put this foolishness to an end. If I need to pay him off or buy out your contract, I'm willing to negotiate, but we can't do that unless one of you calls me back." He didn't relish the idea of drawing a line in the sand, but he was desperate to dictate at least a few rules of this game. "And I want to make sure that neither of you are entertaining any idea of retaliating against Miranda Sterling. If either of you harm a hair on her head, all bets are off. This is about business. Nothing else."

He pressed the red circle on the screen, ending the call. For a moment, he stared at his phone. Thinking. The late-day sun streamed through the window sheers and over his shoulder. His heart began pounding. Had he just made a mistake? Tipped his hand by letting on that Miranda meant something to him?

He sank down onto the couch and ran his hand through his hair. It would all be fine. It had to be. Pietro and his team had eyes on Miranda and her house. She would be safe, and he would fix the problem. Then he could get on with the business of forging a relationship with her and the baby. It might help him come to terms with the death of Johnathon, the brother he'd both loved and hated. It might help him bury so much unhappy history. Right now, it felt like the past was coming back at him, full speed, hell-bent on destroying him from the inside out. He wasn't about to let that happen.

After a long day at her interior-design company, MS Designs, Miranda Sterling was nearly home. She pulled her Range Rover into her La Jolla neighborhood, thoughts fixated on her most pervasive fantasy—a generous bowl of lobster ravioli prepared by her personal chef, followed by a leisurely bubble bath in her enormous soaker tub. Pregnancy had its perks. She was going to take advantage of every one.

She turned into her driveway when her phone rang, the caller ID lighting up the screen—Tara Sterling. Tara was a friend and business partner, but she'd also been the first wife of Johnathon, Miranda's recently deceased husband. Tara and Miranda shared controlling interest of Sterling Enterprises with Astrid, Johnathon's second wife. Johnathon had willed his shares of the company to his three wives, apparently as a testament to how much he'd loved them all. Johnathon had never been anything short of dramatic. "Tara, hey. I just got home. Is this important, or can we talk later? I'm starving and dying to take off these shoes." Miranda eased into the first bay of her four-car garage and killed the engine.

"I'm on my way over to your place with Astrid. We need to talk about Andrew."

Miranda hated the way she kept getting pulled into Sterling Enterprises' drama. Everyone was convinced that Andrew, Johnathon's brother, was somehow meddling in the business. Miranda wasn't convinced. Yes, he and Johnathon had reportedly had a lifelong rivalry, but Andrew didn't seem nearly as evil as people tried to portray him. "What now? We've already talked about this. I have serious doubts about your theory. Do you really think he's the reason there have been so many mistakes on the Seaport Promenade bid?"

"Yes, I do. Astrid and I are almost to your place. We'll talk about it more when we get there."

Miranda didn't love the way Tara and Astrid invited themselves over with very little notice. It was just another sign that everyone knew she had no life beyond work and the baby. Then again, she loved having people over. Tara and Astrid had become true friends, even if it was an unconventional sisterhood. "I hope you like lobster ravioli."

"Are you kidding? I love it."

Miranda made her way inside the house. She'd never get used to how big and empty it felt now that Johnathon was gone. Eight thousand square feet was a silly amount of space for two people to occupy, let alone one person, but she couldn't bring herself to part with their home. It not only had a breathtaking view of the Pacific, but Miranda had also painstakingly decorated every inch of it. The house brought Miranda comfort on the days when she found it hard to dig out from the depths of her grief, and it made her happier whenever she found the courage to simply look ahead to the good things on the horizon, like Thanksgiving, Christmas and, after that, the arrival of her baby girl.

Miranda popped three servings of the ravioli into the oven, thankful she'd had the foresight to ask for extra. Tara and Astrid arrived mere minutes later.

"Come on in." Miranda stepped aside as the two women entered the foyer. Tara, with her bright blond bob and determined stride, led the way, followed by willowy Astrid, the natural beauty and former model. As Miranda closed the door, she couldn't help but notice how she was the short one, especially since she'd kicked off her pumps, while Tara and Astrid were both in heels. At five-seven, Miranda was no shrimp, but the other wives towered over her.

Astrid stooped down and gave Miranda a warm hug. "How are you feeling? Everything good?" Astrid always showed great enthusiasm for the baby on the way, even though she'd suffered years of infertility with Johnathon. Now that she was engaged to Miranda's brother, Clay, Miranda wondered if they would pursue IVF, or perhaps Astrid would choose to focus on becoming a mom to Clay's daughter, Delia.

"I'm mostly just hungry all the time." Miranda waved them both through her spacious living room to the gourmet kitchen, where the heavenly smell of ravioli perfumed the air. "Thankfully, we should be ready to eat in about fifteen minutes. Can I offer either of you a glass of Chablis?" Miranda pulled a bottle from the wine fridge in the center island.

"I'd love one." Astrid perched on one of the barstools.

"Me, too. But I'd really like to address the Andrew situation right away if we can." Tara took a seat next to Astrid.

Miranda cut the foil from the neck of the bottle. "Okay. Shoot."

"He's back in town. I have a friend who saw him at the Grant downtown. I don't think we can wait around to see what he's going to try next," Tara insisted. She then went on to remind Miranda of the misdeeds they were sure he'd committed, including having someone at the city feed misinformation about the project specs to the team at Sterling. "We need to go on the offensive."

Miranda poured two glasses of wine, fighting the frustration she was feeling right now. She'd spent some time with Andrew when he'd come to San Diego a few weeks after Johnathon's death. He might not be perfect, but she didn't see any way he could be the force of evil everyone else seemed to think he was. "I fail to see where I come into all of this. I don't even work at Sterling."

"Exactly why you're the perfect candidate. He won't suspect you," Tara said.

"Plus, you have the best relationship with him. The rest of us don't know him well," Astrid added.

Miranda didn't know Andrew *that* well, but none of the wives did. Andrew hadn't really been a part of Johnathon's life during any of Johnathon's three marriages. Miranda did have the most recent experience with him, and she did like to think she was a good judge of character. There was a part of her that felt a need to clear Andrew's name. "What did you have in mind?"

"Call him and see if you can get together. Try to find out what he's up to."

"He told me he'd reach out if he came back into

town," Miranda said. "He hasn't done that. Maybe there's a reason. Maybe he doesn't want to see me." Why that thought bothered her so much, she wasn't sure.

"Or maybe he's zeroing in on his plan. The city is weeks away from awarding the Seaport contract. If he's trying to meddle with it, he has to act now."

Miranda shook her head. "You all are crazy. I really don't see it."

"Maybe you don't want to see it," Astrid said, sliding her hand across the counter until her fingers brushed Miranda's. "I didn't want to believe it, either, but all evidence points in that direction. I know it's hard. He's our living connection to the man we all loved."

Miranda took in a deep breath. As far as she was concerned, that was a reason to give Andrew the benefit of the doubt. But was she being naive? Johnathon had told her stories about bad things Andrew had done. Vindictive and cruel acts. Of course, Miranda was certain that Johnathon had always countered every mean-spirited jab with one of his own. He'd not been the kind of man who let a punch go unanswered.

No matter what, Miranda wanted to put this topic to rest. If Andrew was innocent, she wanted to be able to say that with certainty. Ultimately, she wanted her child to know as much family as possible. Miranda and her brother, Clay, had no memories of their father. She could not save her daughter that pain, but perhaps it would soften the blow if she was able to have a relationship with her uncle.

"Okay. Fine. I'll call him."

"You will?" Apparently, Tara had anticipated a much bigger fight.

"Yes. I'd like to put this question to rest so we can all move on." Miranda grabbed her phone from the center island and pulled up Andrew's information.

He answered after only a ring or two. "Miranda?"

A noticeable tingle ran down Miranda's back when she heard Andrew's voice. It must be her pregnancy hormones wreaking havoc again. She turned away from Tara and Astrid and wandered closer to the stove on the opposite side of the kitchen. "Andrew, hi. How are you?"

"I'm well. How are you? I'm surprised to hear from you." Again, his voice was warm and soothing, much like the bath she'd been longing for.

Miranda closed her eyes and pinched the bridge of her nose. What she was about to say was going to make her sound like a stalker. "I heard you're in town."

It was so quiet on the other end of the line that Miranda nearly wondered if the connection had dropped. "Who told you that?" His tone was cold and clipped, no longer so comforting.

She had to scramble for an excuse. She couldn't say that Tara and Astrid had provided her with the intel. "I have a friend who saw you. She's the nosy type. I think she assumed that you and I would be seeing each other." Miranda cringed at the sound of that. It was so presumptuous.

"I'm in town on business. I planned to call if I had any free time."

"Oh, of course." Miranda glanced over her shoulder at Tara and Astrid, who were both sitting on the edge of their seats, hanging on Miranda's every word. The pressure was on Miranda to produce. "How long are you here?"

Andrew cleared his throat, making it apparent that she'd put him on the spot. "Not long."

"Would you like to have dinner?" It was the logical invitation. Food was on her mind 24-7. "A man's got to eat, right?"

"I suppose."

"I recently did a full redesign of a steakhouse over in Harbor Island. It has a stunning view of the bay. I haven't had a chance to see the restaurant at night yet."

"Uh, sure. I can do that."

Something about Andrew's inflection made her wonder if he saw this as an imposition. Were Tara and Astrid right? Was Miranda deluded when it came to Andrew? Apparently, she was about to find out. "How about tomorrow night? Meet there at seven?"

Two

Miranda pulled her car up to the valet stand at Harbor Prime, her stomach in knots. Nervousness had been her default setting since she'd ended the call with Andrew yesterday. She was about to do a highwire act without a net. Tara and Astrid were after answers from Andrew on some very difficult questions, while Miranda wanted to continue to forge a genuine connection with him. These objectives were diametrically opposed to each other. How was she supposed to extract sensitive information from Andrew when she would do anything to keep from burning this particular bridge? She had no idea, but she did know one thing for certain—she'd try her hardest to make everyone happy.

She walked inside, immensely pleased with how beautifully the renovation had turned out. Miranda didn't like to brag about her interior-design skills, but she could admit to herself that she'd done an exceptional job on Harbor Prime. The wood beams crisscrossing the high-peaked ceiling were now stained ebony, accenting the island architecture of the building. The booths were upholstered in a gorgeous fabric with a modern botanical print in shades of coffee-brown and grass-green. Of course, the most breathtaking feature of the restaurant was one that Miranda could not take credit for—the view. All along the far wall were floor-to-ceiling windows, which framed the magnificent evening vista of the bay with the city skyline twinkling beyond.

"Ms. Sterling." The hostess stepped out from behind her desk to shake Miranda's hand. "It's nice to have you join us this evening."

"I'm glad I had a chance to come out and see the renovation at night." Miranda scanned the dining room, but didn't see Andrew.

"We have a beautiful table for you this evening, with an exceptional view."

"I don't believe my dinner date is here yet." Miranda felt silly referring to Andrew that way, but it was the first thing that had come out of her mouth.

"Actually, Mr. Sterling arrived ten minutes ago. I went ahead and sat him at your table." The hostess swept her arm forward. "This way."

Miranda followed her through the dining room, which was abuzz with music, heavenly scents and the chatter of happy diners. As they rounded the central bank of booths, Miranda saw him in profile as he looked out over the water. A zap of excitement hit her, doing nothing to settle her nerves. Why would she feel this way? Pregnancy hormones? Or perhaps it was her heart, reminding her that he was so closely linked to the man she'd loved and lost.

Andrew turned and his intense eyes locked on her as he managed a reserved smile. He rose from his seat and she quickly drifted closer when he opened his arms, an invitation she was eager to take. "Miranda, it's good to see you," he muttered into her hair. His embrace was warm and comforting, and there was a part of her that just wanted to stand in his arms for a few hours. It had been so long since she'd felt this good.

"I'm happy to see you, too."

Andrew released and stepped back, noticeably eyeing her belly. "Baby's grown since the last time I saw you."

Miranda resisted the urge to smooth her hands over her stomach. She still wasn't showing much and didn't love the idea of fixating on the ways her body was changing. Being a widow was a vulnerable position, and the pregnancy made it even more so. "I'm just a little more than halfway."

"Pregnancy suits you. You look great." Andrew eased behind her chair and pulled it out for her.

Miranda appreciated the gentlemanly gesture and his kind words more than he ever could have known. It was so nice to be treated well. "Flattery will get you everywhere."

"I'll keep that in mind." Andrew punctuated the end of his sentence with an arch of one eyebrow, then took his seat opposite her. "I haven't ordered a drink yet, but I did ask them to bring you some water. But I don't know if it's filtered, so perhaps we should order something bottled. I know pregnant women need to watch every little thing they eat or drink."

He was so considerate. How anyone could ever suspect him of having unkind motives, Miranda didn't know. "This is just fine, but thank you." Miranda took a sip, her nervousness fading away. She smiled, unable to keep from admiring him. She couldn't help that her inclination was to notice the ways he was like his brother, and the many ways in which they were different. Andrew was remarkably good-looking, like Johnathon, with tousled chestnut-brown hair, but his eyes were a much more complex shade of blue-green. His facial scruff was more pronounced, stopping shy of being an actual beard. The biggest difference was that Andrew had a far more inward demeanor. Nothing about his manner suggested that he needed to be the center of attention, or, quite frankly, that he wanted it that way. That was a massive difference. Johnathon had always insisted on being the sun everyone revolved around.

The server appeared and took their drink orders—a cranberry juice with club soda and lime for Miranda, while Andrew ordered a bourbon neat, delighted that they had a brand called Michter's.

"You don't drink it on the rocks?" Miranda asked.

"Not this one. It's small-batch. Too delicious to water down."

"I see."

Andrew's sights settled on Miranda's face, and for a moment, she had the nerve to return the look, if only to peer into the storm of his eyes, hoping for clues as to who he really was or what he wanted. She'd heard so many stories from Johnathon, none of which cast Andrew in a positive light. Sitting here, just the two of them, it was hard to envision him doing anything evil or underhanded. But Miranda broke their shared gaze when she started to feel nervous again. She turned her attention to the water, just as the server delivered their drinks.

"Cheers," Andrew offered, raising his glass.

"To family." Her toast made her want to cast aside the true nature of her visit. This should be a time for building the bond between them, not extracting information.

He closed his eyes for an instant as he enjoyed a sip of bourbon, then swirled it in his glass as he again gazed at her with such intensity that it made her feel as though she was under a microscope. She had to wonder what he saw when he looked at her. Was she a friend to him? Merely his brother's wife, and therefore, an obligation? The fact that he hadn't called to let her know he was in town seemed to suggest she was an afterthought. And she couldn't ignore that he'd hesitated to accept her invitation.

Andrew opened his menu. "Any suggestions?"

Miranda snapped back to the moment and turned her thoughts to her favorite subject of late—food. "It's all good. They have an excellent wedge salad to start and they'll bring warm popovers to the table. Beyond that, the steaks are amazing and prepared to perfection. You seriously can't go wrong."

He nodded and closed his menu. "Perfect. Have you decided? We should order."

"Do you have somewhere you need to be?"

"I have some business to attend to later tonight."

That seemed strange. "That works for me. Food is a big priority right now." A breathy laugh left her lips. "It's all I think about. That and sleeping."

He turned to look over his shoulder, flagging their server. "Let's get you taken care of. My brother's not here to do it, so I will." A hush fell between them, even though the noisiness of the restaurant remained.

Miranda felt like she was adrift at sea, all by herself. It had been a familiar feeling since Johnathon's death, but she hoped she wouldn't have to live with it forever.

Andrew reached out his right hand for Miranda's

left, which was resting on the table. His warm palm blanketed her fingers, including the one where her wedding rings still sat. "I'm sorry. I shouldn't have said that. It was incredibly insensitive."

"Andrew. It's fine. My loss is your loss. There's no way around that."

Their server arrived at the table. "Are we ready to order?"

Andrew dropped his head ever so slightly, seeking Miranda's approval. "Ready?"

"Yes. Absolutely." She rattled off a few favorites, her mouth watering at the idea of the meal ahead. Andrew followed.

"Perfect," the server said. "I'll put this in right away."

They were left alone again, and that meant Miranda's nerves returned. She wanted the uneasiness to go away, so she and Andrew could enjoy their meal together. Which meant she needed to move forward with her objective, get her answers and put the whole thing to rest. She was unsure of how to bring up the subject of Andrew meddling in Sterling Enterprises, but thought the direct approach was best. "Now that we're able to chat in person, there's something I'm curious about." She shifted in her seat, struggling to utter the question she had to ask. *Just come out with it so you can get past this.* "Did you come back to town because you have an interest in the Seaport Promenade project?"

* * *

Michter's twenty-year bourbon was not meant to be slugged back. It was meant to be savored. Still, Andrew considered downing it in one gulp, if only to take off the edge of the moment and calculate his next move. Unfortunately, Miranda's question put him on unsteady ground, while her beauty was a distraction that knocked him off his feet. Her warm brown eyes, while painted with uncertainty, were mesmerizing. Her dark, glossy hair softly framed her flawless face and fell across her shoulders in a luscious cascade. No wonder Johnathon had been drawn to her. It was impossible to look away. And yet, Andrew had to. She wasn't his to admire.

He couldn't ignore what she'd asked and he had no business expressing surprise that she'd figured this out. She struck him as incredibly smart and she was reportedly quite tangled up with Sterling Enterprises business now that she had a direct stake. Part of him wanted to brush aside his misdeeds for now, hide them until he'd had a chance to make everything better. But another part of him was exhausted from living under the guilt of secrets.

"How much do you know?" he asked, buying himself more time.

"How much do you want to tell me?"

Andrew could literally be here for hours, detailing every little thing that had happened between Johnathon and him that ultimately led to the decision to interfere with Sterling. But he wasn't about to air his grievances over dinner. "I did take an interest in the Seaport Promenade project. Specifically, an interest in preventing Johnathon from landing the deal."

"I see." She took a sip of her drink and ran her slender fingers around the base of the glass, then she set it back down on the table. Everything about Miranda was beautiful, but something about her hands was particularly enchanting. "And does that mean you took an active role in keeping it from happening?"

"Yes. I did. It was my idea."

She drew a breath in through her nose and her jaw tensed. She didn't seem like a woman who might make a scene, but in that moment, he could see the possibility. "Why would you do that? To your own brother?" Her voice wobbled ever so slightly, but her posture remained determined. She wasn't going to back down until Andrew gave up more of the information he'd worked so hard to hide.

"Surely he told you about our relationship. Surely he told you how little he liked me."

"He told me that you two never got along. He told me you were capable of being underhanded, which I really didn't want to believe once we'd finally met and had a chance to talk."

It confounded him that she had any inclination to give him the benefit of the doubt. No one did that. He didn't even do it for himself. It was a foolish pursuit. "It's true, though. I've done bad things."

"And I've been defending you to people at Sterling. Please don't tell me I made a mistake."

So it wasn't merely Miranda's suspicion that he was interfering with the Seaport project. The powers that be at Sterling were apparently aware of his scheme, as well. "I never gave you any reason to have any faith in me."

"That's not true. We had an amazing conversation that night you came to see me a few weeks after Johnathon died. I didn't know what to expect, but you were truly torn up about his death."

Memories of that night, which was the first time he and Miranda had met, flooded his brain. Little else had occupied his thoughts since then. He'd gone to her house expecting the worst—screaming and yelling and possibly kicking him out. After all, he'd done the unthinkable and skipped his own brother's funeral. He'd been unwilling to face their history, or the reality that this person who had consumed so much of his life, his brother, was gone.

But he'd ultimately let guilt dictate his actions and had reached out to Miranda in person. Everything hit him at once that night—she was pregnant with his niece or nephew, a child who would never have a relationship with his deceased brother. And Andrew was making an innocent baby's predicament worse by trying to drag Johnathon's business and reputation through the mud. That was the moment when he'd known he had to put a stop to his plan.

"I heard it in your voice that night when you talked about Johnathon," Miranda continued. "Whatever happened between you two, I believe you loved each other. I know it. That's all I care about."

Was that really true? Andrew wasn't sure. Right now, he was more concerned with a man at the bar who'd glanced over his shoulder in Andrew and Miranda's direction. The situation with Victor had him on high alert. "I'm sorry for having a plan in the first place. I had my reasons, but none of that matters now." He sat back in his seat and took another generous sip of his bourbon. "If I could do it all over again, I would never have set these particular wheels in motion."

Miranda sucked in a deep breath, seeming to run through everything he had just said. Meanwhile, their salads were delivered, along with the fresh popovers. She tore apart the yeasty, puffy bread as soon as she could, adding a dollop of butter. She popped a bite into her mouth then licked her bottom lip, where a drop of butter had been left behind. The vision left Andrew stuck. She was beguiling. And he needed to stop looking.

"Thank God there's food. This conversation is making me anxious." Miranda dabbed at her mouth with a napkin.

Indeed, the popovers were warm and comforting, and a welcome respite from the topic at hand. "I agree."

"Look, I'm not trying to get you to tell me everything about your issues with Johnathon. It's obvious that it's not something you want to talk about, and the truth is that he's not here to answer for any of it. I think it's most fair to you, and to him, if we just let it go. But I have one thing I want. I want you to stop."

"I want to, but it's not that simple." Again, the man at the bar stole another glance at them. He was tempted to ask Miranda if she knew him, but he didn't want to draw attention to what might potentially be a problem. If things got dicey, he'd keep her safe.

"From where I'm sitting, it's incredibly simple. You're the only living connection I have to Johnathon. You're the baby's only biological relative on her father's side. You should be a part of her life. But that can't happen if you're threatening her birthright with this scheme."

"Her?"

"Yes." A smile bloomed across her stunning face. "A little girl."

Every passing minute with Miranda brought Andrew's misdeeds into sharper focus. In his mind's eye, he could see his future niece. Hurting her was unthinkable. And here was her mother, with every reason to be angry with him, and she was inviting him into their life. The idea stole his breath away.

"That's why I'm here in San Diego. To stop the plan."
I have to.

Miranda's eyes narrowed on him. "Then just do it."

Their entrées had arrived, but Andrew didn't have much appetite anymore. "I had a partner. A man named Victor. You have to understand that Johnathon had a lot of enemies, and I'd put Victor near the top of the list. He jumped at the chance to take part. But after Johnathon died, I told Victor we had to stop. Unfortunately, he didn't agree. So now he's gone rogue and I have to track him down if I have any chance of convincing him to end it."

Her face clouded with confusion. "If he's here in San Diego, you should just let me talk to him. I can be pretty persuasive."

Andrew had zero doubt about that. Andrew nearly laughed at her willingness to trust others. It struck him as brave, but horribly naive. He wasn't going to let her within fifty feet of Victor, especially while she was pregnant. "I'm the only one who can stop him." Andrew again saw the man at the bar look in their direction. There was no way he was merely another customer. Something was going on.

"That sounds like something Johnathon would say. You should let me help you. This is in my interest, too."

"Please. Miranda. This is between me and Victor." *And the ghost of your dead husband.* "It might require a few concessions, but I'll get it done. I promise."

Miranda shook her head while enjoying a bite of her steak. "I will never understand the games men play in business, especially when you get to be as rich as you are. You've already won. Can't you just be satisfied?"

She was so right. If only he'd had a Miranda in his life to steer him straight. Things might have turned out differently. But love hadn't been kind to Andrew. Not like it had been to Johnathon. "We're ridiculous, aren't we? We hoard our toys and don't want to share with anyone."

She pointed at him with her fork. "Exactly. That's how Johnathon was. Always on the lookout for the next kill. He took entirely too much pleasure in beating others."

Andrew knew that very well. He'd been on the receiving end too many times to count. "My brother was very good at it. It's hard not to keep going when you excel at something."

Miranda shrugged. "I guess. It still doesn't mean I understand the need to be ruthless."

"Of course you don't. You're a kind person. You clearly have a generous heart. I appreciate that you want me to be a part of your life and the baby's. It means more to me than you know."

"Family is incredibly important to me, and I don't have much. I have to hold on to everyone I can."

She was so beautiful and pure of heart. He wasn't sure he deserved to sit at the same table with her, let alone be part of her life. "I understand. I'm in a similar situation."

"Right. Which means you and I need to stick together. And that starts right now. You should not be staying at a hotel. It isn't right. Family stays with family. You should come stay with me."

His pulse picked up, pounding in his ears. He had no business getting physically closer to Miranda. She'd only distract him from the task at hand. "No. Thank you."

"You're turning me down?"

I'm keeping you safe. "I don't want to be an inconvenience."

"It's no trouble at all. I'm in that big empty house by myself all the time. It gets really lonely. And boring. You'd be doing me a favor. It would be so nice just to have someone else there."

Andrew scrambled for another argument to make. He was already fighting an attraction that was all wrong. Spending more time with Miranda would only make it worse.

Their server appeared at the table. "Are we still working on the meal?"

"Wow. I pretty well polished that off, didn't I?" Miranda asked, then pointed to Andrew's plate, which was still half-full. "Is everything okay?"

"I'm fine," Andrew said. "Just too caught up in our conversation."

"I have a piece of Mississippi mud pie coming out from the kitchen for you in a moment," the server said. "The gentleman at the bar sent it over." She turned and gestured in that direction, but then her expression fell. "Oh. I guess he left."

"Did you see someone you know?" Andrew asked Miranda, desperately hoping the answer was yes.

She shook her head. "I don't think so. But dessert sure sounds good."

The hair on the back of Andrew's neck stood up. He'd thought that man was suspicious. Was this Victor's way of letting Andrew know that he was close by? He wasn't about to let on about his suspicions. "It does."

The server left and Andrew took the chance to finish his bourbon. He had to remind himself that he could handle this. He could take care of Victor. So why was he feeling so especially nervous about it? Probably because of the pregnant woman sitting across the table from him.

"Well? What do you think about my offer? Coming to stay at the house?" Miranda asked.

Andrew knew this wasn't a good idea. He was already saddled with unbearable guilt over the plan he'd set in motion. Having to fight his attraction to his dead brother's wife was only going to make setting things right a more complicated proposition.

But he couldn't worry about his own internal struggles. He was stronger than that. Bottom line, he had to keep Miranda safe. Johnathon would expect it of him. "It sounds great. I'd love to accept the invitation."

Three

"Moving in? With you? Into your house?" Tara asked Miranda, her voice booming over the phone line.

Miranda winced at the line of questions. Everything about them was bad. The tone. The substance. The volume. "He's not moving in. He's coming to stay with me for a few nights. People do that, you know. Families." Miranda peered out the window, waiting on Andrew's arrival.

"He's not your family."

"What are you talking about? He's Johnathon's brother. He will be biologically related to my child. That's family." She tugged the curtain back into place and wandered into the living room, plopping down in a chair.

"Family sticks around. Family goes to the funeral when someone passes away."

"He and Johnathon were estranged. That happens. I could spend my entire life resenting Andrew for his mistake, or I can move on with my life. I'm inclined to do the latter. This hasn't been easy for me." It was the truth. Losing her husband while expecting their child had been one of the most difficult things Miranda had ever endured. It was a never-ending tug-of-war between the grief over what was lost and the hope over what was to be. She had to lean toward the more optimistic side of her circumstances. It was the only way to stay sane.

"Well, Grant and I are very concerned." It came as no surprise that Tara's fiancé, Grant, didn't like this idea. He'd been Johnathon's oldest friend. "Not only are you letting the man who was secretly sabotaging Sterling Enterprises into your home, he accepted the invitation. What is he after?"

Miranda sighed. She trusted Andrew. If that made her a fool, so be it. At least she could say that she'd tried to build a bridge to him. "I told you. He's in town to track down this Victor person."

"Grant doesn't know who Victor is. That seems highly suspicious. Grant knew about all of Johnathon's business dealings, and he knows everyone who hated him. I think Andrew is lying."

Miranda was not the sort of woman who convinced herself of things that weren't true, but she did feel as though she saw qualities in Andrew that no one else did. Perhaps it was her charge to show others the light. "Andrew didn't try to hide his plan from me. He came right out and owned up to it. He apologized. Why would he do that if he had ulterior motives?"

"That's the thing about hidden agendas. They're hidden."

Miranda choked back a grumble of frustration. "I really don't think he was being dishonest, okay? Can we leave it at that?"

"What does your brother think?"

Clay had shown some reservation, but that was normal for him. He was immensely protective of Miranda, just as he was of his daughter, Delia, and now his fiancée, Astrid, the second of the Sterling wives. In the end, Miranda had convinced Clay that this was the right thing and that he had nothing to worry about. "He's fine with it."

"Really?" The incredulity in Tara's voice was unmistakable.

"Yes." Miranda heard the sound of a car door closing outside. "I have to go, Tara."

"I hope you know that I'm only being a pain because I care about you and the baby. You're like a sister to me."

Miranda felt utterly stuck between the people she

cared the most about—Tara, Clay and Grant on one side, and Andrew on the other. "I know your heart's in the right place. You have to trust that mine is, too."

"Please tell me you'll call me if there's a problem."

"I will." She ended the call and got out of the chair, taking her time ambling to the front door. She didn't want to appear too eager. She wasn't sure how she was supposed to feel about his arrival. She was excited by the prospect of having some company and no longer being alone in this house. But she was unsure what their dynamic would be like. Between the things Johnathon had said and Miranda's own experiences, Andrew was still an unknown quantity.

She turned the latch and opened her front door just as Andrew was climbing out of a big black SUV. She couldn't help but notice the way her heart flipped at the sight of him in dark jeans, a black dress shirt with the sleeves rolled up and black sunglasses. He might be an enigma, but he was wrapped up in a far-too-appealing package. Andrew was more than handsome. He was ridiculously hot. Smoking. Was she just supposed to ignore that while they were living under the same roof?

"I didn't expect a welcoming committee." He waved to Miranda as he strode up to her front steps, toting a brown leather men's overnight bag.

"I wouldn't want to be a bad host." She was proud of herself for speaking, fighting her true inclination to bite down on her lower lip.

Andrew cupped her shoulder and leaned down to kiss her cheek, leaving behind a warmth that radiated through her body. "How are you?"

Dizzy. "Good. You?"

"Glad to be out of the hotel. I'll tell you that much."

"Good. Come on in." With a deep breath, Miranda composed herself and made her way inside. Andrew followed, closing the door behind him. "I'll show you up to your room so you can drop your bag and get settled," she said.

"Please. Lead the way."

She traipsed through the wide central hall, past the living room and kitchen to the left and her home office on the right. When they reached the stairs and started the climb to the second floor, she was overcome by a heightened awareness of his presence behind her. With each step, they were venturing closer to privacy and solitude, where absolutely anything might happen. The realization set off a conflict between her body and brain. She was undeniably attracted to Andrew. Her immediate physical reaction could not be questioned. But he was her dead husband's brother. It wasn't right for her to have desirous feelings toward him. It was wrong, bad, and terribly inappropriate. How would she ever reconcile the battle between her wants and what was sensible?

Stop it. You're thinking like Tara. Miranda was not going to let worry rule her life. With a baby on the way, there was already plenty to feel unsure of. Andrew was a wonderful man, but totally off-limits. The time had come for her to strengthen their relationship—to get close, but not *too* close.

Down the hall, she arrived at one of her three guest rooms. Johnathon had always liked having people around, and there had been many times when the house was fully occupied by various friends from all over the world. Those memories were part of what made the present state of her home so unsettling. It was entirely too empty and quiet.

"Here you are," Miranda said, stepping inside and flipping on the light.

"It's perfect." Andrew set his bag next to the dresser. "Did you design this room? It's spectacular."

Heat rose in her cheeks. She was proud of the job she'd done on this room. It was the most masculine of the guest spaces, with charcoal-gray bedding and a faux parchment treatment on the wall behind the bed. Over each of the dark wood bedside tables was a dramatic pendant light fixture hanging from the ten-foot ceiling. This room was magnificent at night. "I did the whole house."

Andrew set down his sunglasses on one of the tables, then turned and offered a faint smile. "I'm duly impressed."

If anyone was blown away, it was Miranda. Everything about Andrew was a deluge to the senses—his warm and citrusy smell, his affable grin and the genuine mystery of his eyes. It made her appreciate his presence that much more, but she reminded herself that this was temporary. It was best not to fixate on his many selling points. "I'm glad you're here."

"I'm thankful for the invitation."

"How long do you think you'll stay?"

"Not too long. A few days? A week? I'll head back to Seattle as soon as I wrap things up with Victor."

"You won't be able to stay for Thanksgiving? It's less than two weeks away." She heard the disappointment in her own voice and knew she had to dial it back. It wasn't her place to put expectations on him. "I mean, it would be nice if you could be here for it. I'm hosting. My brother will be here with Astrid and his daughter. Grant and Tara."

"I doubt I'll need to be here that long."

Perhaps holidays weren't important to Andrew the way they were to Miranda. She clung to them because they signaled the normalcy she hadn't always had in her life. "Sounds like you're ready to get to work then. Will you need an office space? I could set you up in Johnathon's study."

He cleared his throat and his posture stiffened. "I don't know if that's a good idea. I wouldn't want to intrude on your memories of him. I'm sure that room means a lot to you."

"Honestly, I haven't stepped foot in there since he died. I'm sure that sounds crazy, but I couldn't bring myself to do it. I think it would be nice if someone actually used it. Then it wouldn't have to be a place for thinking about loss. It could just be a functioning room."

Andrew stuffed his hands into his pants pockets. "I don't know."

Miranda didn't intend to push Andrew to do something he didn't want to do, but she also sensed that he hadn't come to terms with Johnathon's death. Perhaps this would help him along. "Come on. I'll let you check it out."

"Okay. If nothing else, I'd like to see it."

Together they walked to the very end of the hall and to Johnathon's study. Miranda wasn't quite sure why she hadn't ventured inside after Johnathon was gone, aside from her fear of sinking into the depths of a sadness from which she might never return. She'd had her days of running her hands through Johnathon's clothes in the closet or smelling his cologne. Doing those things hadn't made her feel any better, and certainly hadn't brought him back. So why make it worse by going into the room where he'd spent so much time?

The office was exactly as Johnathon had left it—neat as a pin. Not so much as a stray piece of paper had been left out. There was the mahogany desk Miranda had spent months hunting for, an impossibly heavy antique, and a collection of vintage maps of San Diego and Southern California, to remind him of his love of the area. And, of course, there was an entire wall devoted to the many awards and pieces of publicity Johnathon had earned in his relatively short time on earth—businessman of the year, philanthropic accolades, magazine covers.

"It's a stunning room," Andrew said, noticeably not venturing past the threshold. "My brother was a very lucky guy."

"He definitely had a way of bending the universe to his will, didn't he?" Miranda stepped inside, hoping that would make Andrew come along, but he remained in the doorway. She could see the trepidation on his face, the way he was unsure of himself, which was such a stark contrast to his usual confident stance. Was it because this room was as close to a confrontation with his brother as he might ever get?

"He sure did."

"Do you want to tell me more about what happened between you two? Or are you going to stay vague about it, the way Johnathon did?"

Before he answered the question, Andrew had to remind himself of the entire reason he was back in town and now found himself in Miranda's house. He was here to keep her safe and to meet the opportunity she'd put before him—to become a part of her life and her daughter's. This was a delicate proposition and he wasn't about to mess it up. He wanted to be closer to Miranda. But she was his brother's widow, and if ever there was a woman he needed to see as off-limits, it was her. He would not step into his brother's shoes.

Still, he'd gotten sucked right into Miranda's sweet disposition as soon as he'd walked through the door, and now he was having to deal with that while confronted with an uncomfortable presence— the specter of his brother. It was all around him, this entire room a testament to his accomplishments and the many ways he'd triumphed, with Miranda at the heart of it all.

"You're about to have his baby, Miranda. You were his wife. I don't want my past with him to color the way you see him. It's not fair to him. And it's not fair to me, either, to be honest. I wouldn't exactly be a good houseguest if I came in and told you stories about how Johnathon and I were rivals, or how he always seemed to get everything right and I was the one who made the mistakes."

"He wasn't perfect. There's no need to worry about keeping him on a pedestal."

He still wasn't convinced. "Speaking ill of the dead is never a good idea."

"I understand what you're saying, but I've learned things since he died that were a total shock to the system." Her eyes darted from side to side as if she was searching for something, but eventually she seemed to put it all together. "Wait a minute. You already know what I'm talking about, don't you? The secret he hid from me?"

"No. I don't know a thing."

"But you orchestrated it. The email I got. The Sterling Enterprises IT department traced it back to your company. It was all part of the plan to disrupt the business at Sterling, wasn't it?" Much like she had at dinner last night, she was becoming more and more upset. The color rose in her cheeks, while her eyes were full of pain he didn't fully understand.

"I didn't send any email, Miranda. I honestly don't have any idea what you're alluding to."

"I got a message from Johnathon's work account. It said he slept with Astrid, his second wife, after he and I got engaged. It was written like it came from Johnathon, but that part was just a cruel joke. Unfortunately, Astrid confirmed that it was all true. I think the information was leaked by a woman named Sandy, who worked at Sterling. If you don't know about it, does that mean she's connected to Victor?"

Andrew felt the blood go cold in his veins. This was a lot to unpack—his brother had betrayed Miranda, but the news had been delivered by Victor, courtesy of his heartless ways. It made one thing very clear for Andrew—his true loyalty needed to be to Miranda. She was the person with the most to lose, who had been hurt the most. "I'm so sorry Johnathon cheated on you. I had no idea." He took no pleasure in seeing this chink in his brother's perfect facade. It had come at too high a price for Miranda.

She wrapped her arms around her middle, as if

she could shield herself from the world. "There's nothing I can do about it. What's done is done. I've come to terms with it."

"It's still a terrible betrayal."

"It is, but it's also an instance in which your brother was not perfect. So whatever it is that you think you need to live up to, I promise you that you can stop trying to compete."

Andrew sighed and finally found the nerve to step into the room. It felt a bit like he was confronting the spirit of his brother, but right now, Andrew's most important task was to comfort Miranda. He pulled her into his arms and held her tight. "It's not about me right now."

"So it wasn't you who orchestrated the message? The email?"

"No." He stood back slightly and peered down into her flawless face. Her eyes were watery, like she was on the verge of tears. No, he hadn't been responsible for this, but he'd put the actors in place. "But I did hire the woman who leaked the information. Sandy. I put her in place at Sterling. It's just that she went to work for Victor after I tried to put an end to the plan."

"And what was her role in all of this?"

"She was the mole inside Sterling."

"She was hired as Johnathon's new assistant. You put her right in the lion's den."

Go big or go home. "That was a lucky break. It

could have gone a different way. The plan was always to have someone there to interfere with Sterling's bid to redevelop the Seaport Promenade. She was there to create mistakes so they couldn't land it."

"Why that project? From what I understand, there are plenty of deals with far bigger profits. It seems like it's all about bragging rights."

Andrew wasn't about to answer her question fully, but he could at least give her the framework for his theory. "It was significant to me, and that made it of importance to Johnathon. The fact that there's so little profit to be made only seems to prove that he pursued it for personal reasons. To not only put a knife in my back, but to twist it."

"What could possibly be so important about the promenade that it would cause this much trouble between you?"

"It's a symbol of the city. This is where we grew up, and where we both tried to make a life for ourselves. Johnathon succeeded at building an empire here. I didn't." Andrew sucked in a deep breath and forced himself to stop. He didn't want her pity, and he didn't want to crack open his own heart in front of her, either. "Johnathon and I were engaged in a lifelong game of king of the hill. It felt like this was his attempt to permanently plant a victory flag on top of the mountain."

Miranda shook her head slowly, seeming unsatisfied with his answer. "Why do I feel like you still aren't telling me everything?"

Because I'm not. "Did you ever know him to be petty or vindictive?"

She bunched up her lips like she was having to think very hard about this. "Not toward me, but I heard stories."

"Some of those stories were right. That's why Victor wants to carry out the plan. He and Johnathon had a bad business deal. Victor feels that he bore the brunt of the loss. He doesn't care at all about the Seaport project, but he does care about damaging Sterling's reputation and sabotaging the company."

"But Johnathon's gone. He'll just be hurting innocent people. There's no more revenge to get now, is there?"

Miranda saw it so clearly, but it hadn't been that simple for Andrew. Even in the shock of Johnathon's death, he'd been blinded by the memories of his brother, a lifetime of conflict that had shaped nearly every circumstance of Andrew's existence. "I know. You're right. But there's no telling Victor that." Just thinking about it made him even more eager to fix the mess he'd made. He had to redouble his efforts to reach Victor and get him to pull the plug.

"Maybe I should be grateful for it. It brought you back to San Diego. We wouldn't have had this time together otherwise."

What made Miranda so trusting and pure of

heart? Andrew couldn't imagine what it might be like to go through life like that. He wasn't sure if he was wired this way, or if it was the result of a lifetime of betrayal, but he felt destined to never put his faith in anyone. "That's a very sunny way of looking at the situation."

"Or it's desperate. I'm clinging to everything and everyone I have."

The idea of her holding on to him made him that much more resolute to fix the problem he'd created. He would not leave her with anything less than what she deserved.

"You must be hungry. Would you like some lunch?"

"You've already done so much. Let me cook for you?"

Miranda cocked an eyebrow at him. "Seriously? I don't think your brother knew how to operate the stove."

"You must realize by now that we're very different people."

"I'm starting to see that, but there are similarities. I see him in you."

Andrew needed to continue to set himself apart. He didn't want his identity and that of his brother too closely linked. "If it's all the same to you, I'd like to focus on the differences."

Four

Andrew had made it through his first week living with Miranda without doing anything stupid. That felt like a big win. By day, he worked out of her house, utilizing Johnathon's study. By night, they enjoyed time together. They even managed to largely avoid the topic of Johnathon, even though his brother was a looming presence in the house. Andrew seemed to make Miranda happy by preparing dinner every night, and that, in turn, filled him with a satisfaction that was growing by the day. But he knew that the pleasure he took in being around her was ultimately not good. He couldn't afford to get too comfortable. His life in Seattle was waiting for him—a lonely existence, but one in which the only risks he took were with business.

Unfortunately, he'd made no progress on the Victor front. He'd left countless messages. He'd sent Pietro on several trips to various locales around the city where they might be able to find him. Victor was hiding, lurking somewhere in the shadows, and that could only mean bad things. Andrew had also attempted to reach Sandy with a similar result. He suspected that money was at the root of her loyalty, and if that was all it would take to get her to end her involvement, he'd give her whatever she wanted.

It was late Friday afternoon when Miranda's doorbell rang, and Andrew went to answer it. A burly delivery guy was waiting outside, with a truck parked behind him.

"I have a delivery for Miranda Sterling." The man handed over a clipboard.

Andrew looked at the shipping order. It was from a furniture company, which made little sense. Wouldn't she have that shipped to her office? "Before I sign for it, I need to call Ms. Sterling and make sure this is okay." How was he supposed to know this wasn't Victor sending another signal that he was watching Andrew and Miranda?

The man grunted. "I have other deliveries to make."

"I'm sure you do. One minute." Andrew turned

his back and pulled his cell out of his pocket to call Miranda.

"Hey there. Is everything okay?" she asked.

"Yes. Everything is fine. I wanted to see if you were expecting a delivery from a company called Bella Furniture."

"Oh, my God. That's the crib. It wasn't supposed to arrive until the middle of December. Yes. Please sign for it." The excitement in her voice was unmistakable, and it gave him a lift he hadn't expected.

He cradled the phone between his ear and shoulder while turning back to the front door and signing for the shipment.

"You want me to bring it inside?" the driver asked.

"Yes. Please." Andrew returned his attention to Miranda, but he watched as another delivery person began wheeling the crate to the door. "It looks like a flat box. Does it need to be assembled?"

"It does, but I'll have one of the guys from my warehouse come to the house and do it."

"Why don't you let me handle it?" He waved the deliverymen inside, and they hauled the oversize box into the foyer.

"That's not necessary. You're busy."

He didn't want to tell her that he felt utterly useless since he'd been unable to achieve his primary objective while in San Diego—stopping Victor. "I'd really like to do this for you. And the baby. Please."

"Okay," she said. "If you insist."

"I insist." He found himself smiling. It felt so damn good to make her happy.

"While I have you on the phone, I wanted to let you know that my brother, Clay, is coming by the house in a little bit. He has his own key, but I thought I should give you a heads-up. His daughter, Delia, left one of her favorite books at my house the last time they were over. She's been asking for it for over a week."

"Okay. Great. I look forward to meeting him."

"Sounds good. I'll see you when I get home."

Andrew ended the call, overcome by the feelings of comfort Miranda gave him. He reminded himself not to become accustomed to this. This wasn't his life.

The box was simply too big to carry upstairs, so Andrew cracked it open and began ferrying the parts up the stairs and to the nursery. With every trip, he thought a bit more about what was ahead for Miranda, raising a baby on her own. He supposed that she would have the help of her brother, so it wasn't like she'd be without a safety net, but it still made him wish there was a place for him somewhere in the midst of that. Perhaps more regular visits would be in order. But only if that was what Miranda wanted.

After six or seven trips upstairs, the doorbell rang again. Andrew answered, coming face-to-face with Clay, Miranda's brother, for the first time.

"Miranda told me you'd probably be here. Clay

Morgan." Clay extended his hand. He had the same dark hair as Miranda, but a decidedly more intense demeanor.

Andrew shook Clay's hand and opened the door wider. "Please. Come in."

"I won't be in your way for long. I think the book I'm looking for is in Miranda's office," Clay said.

"You're welcome to stay if you want. I'm just unpacking the crib Miranda ordered for the nursery."

"Really? Can I help?"

"Yeah. Of course." Who was Andrew to say no? Plus, he relished the chance to get to know Miranda's brother. "Just grab whatever you want. Most of it is already upstairs."

Between the two of them, they were able to bring up the final pieces in a single trip. "Are you planning on putting it together?"

Andrew surveilled the pile of parts, wooden panels and hardware. "Believe it or not, yes."

"I assembled my daughter's crib when she was born and let me tell you, it's much easier if you have two people. I'd be happy to help."

"You sure you don't need to go? I don't want to keep you from your family."

Clay consulted his watch. "I'll help you for an hour. Astrid is at work and Delia's with the nanny, so I definitely have time."

"Great. I'd appreciate it."

The pair went to work, Clay organizing the parts

and Andrew reading the instructions after gathering some tools from Miranda's utility room.

"How long are you in town?" Clay asked as they started the assembly.

"I'd originally thought only a few days, but my work project isn't quite coming together the way I thought it would."

"You mean dismantling your plan to take down the company I work for?"

Whoa. Andrew hadn't quite expected that, but he admired Clay's candor. "In a word, yes. I don't know how much Miranda told you."

"She gave me the highlights. For what it's worth, I appreciate that you're willing to fix your own mess. Not enough people are like that. Most people hide from their mistakes."

Andrew was starting to think that kindness might just run in the Morgan family. Clay seemed as generous as his sister. "Don't give me too much credit. I still messed up pretty bad."

"I don't have a brother, so I can't really relate to whatever rivalry you had with Johnathon, but I do understand how intense a relationship with a sibling can be. I can see how it might motivate you to do some crazy things."

"You love your sister a lot, don't you?"

Clay looked right at Andrew. "I do. Absolutely. Which is why I'm rooting for you to be able to save Sterling Enterprises from any ill effects of whatever it is this Victor person plans to do. If you hurt the company, you hurt her. And the baby. It's the glue that brings us all together."

Andrew felt the weight of the moment squarely on his shoulders. He would not let Miranda down. He couldn't. "Don't worry. I've already promised Miranda that I won't let anything bad happen. Nothing at all."

Miranda had a hard time concentrating after she got off the phone with Andrew. The fact that he'd offer to drop everything and assemble the crib? Well, that was just too much. Once again, she failed to see the bad person others seemed to think he was. In fact, quite the opposite. She saw only good.

As a result, she found herself unable to focus as the rest of the workday ticked away, all in anticipation of the moment she could leave the office and spend the weekend with Andrew. She knew she shouldn't be getting attached, but she couldn't help it. After their first week together, it was clear that Andrew and Miranda had little trouble coexisting. They had breakfast together each morning, then went their separate ways, Miranda to her office and Andrew into Johnathon's study, where he managed his development firm from a distance, all while trying to track down the mysterious Victor. In the evening, they were drawn back together for dinner, which Andrew insisted on making. He enjoyed cooking.

He said it relaxed him and that he liked doing something nice for her.

Every minute they spent together made Miranda doubt the opinion so many people seemed to hold of Andrew. He was not conniving, nor was he vengeful or even mean-spirited. It even had her questioning the picture Johnathon had painted of his brother. Perhaps they had been different together, although she'd never know. That opportunity was gone now. It saddened her to think about what might have been if the brothers had found a way to reconcile before one of them was gone.

She arrived home from work a little after 6:00 p.m. A last-minute panic from one of her clients meant that she'd left later than she wanted to. Just as she pulled into the garage, she got a text from Clay. I met Andrew. Super nice guy. Talk soon?

She was relieved to know that someone else liked Andrew. She wasn't imagining things. Great. And yes. We need to talk about Thanksgiving.

I'll call you this weekend.

She tossed her phone back into her bag and walked inside. "Hello?" she called out into the house.

"Up here in the nursery," Andrew shouted back.

She cast aside her purse and hurried down the hall and up the stairs. As soon as she reached the landing, she spotted Andrew wearing jeans, a T-shirt and a big smile, standing outside the baby's room.

He looked good enough to eat. And she needed to stop seeing him that way. She considered trying to convince him to wear baggier clothes, but she wasn't sure that was going to help. *Enjoy it while you can. He's not here forever.* "How's it going?" she asked.

"It's done," he announced with more than a hint of excitement in his voice.

"It is?"

"To be fair, your brother helped me."

She couldn't ignore the way his shirt clung to his strong shoulders and sculpted chest. "I can't wait to see it." She tried to take a peek inside the nursery, but Andrew stopped her with both hands on her shoulders.

"Hold on. You don't get to look yet."

"Why not? My baby, my house, my rules."

Andrew shook his head with a hint of mischief in his eyes. "Indulge me. I'd like you to be surprised by my hard work."

"I thought my brother helped."

"Okay. I guess it's our work. Now close your eyes."

She did as she was told, which made the anticipation of this moment that much more urgent. She was dying to see what the baby's room was going to look like. She'd seen it in her mind's eye many times, but it was all about to become that much more real. Andrew held on to one shoulder and she sensed him moving. Sure enough, there was a hand on her other shoulder a moment later. He was standing behind her, close enough that she could feel his body warmth.

"I'm going to walk you inside. It's just about three steps, straight ahead." His voice was soft against her ear, sending tingles through her body.

"Okay." She took the first step and Andrew began to count.

"One…"

Another two steps.

"Two. Three."

"Can I open my eyes?"

"Yes. Go."

She did it slowly, the room coming into focus and then just as quickly going fuzzy from tears. Ahead sat the crib, in exactly the spot where she'd envisioned it, which was amazing considering she hadn't told Andrew where it belonged. It was even more beautiful than she'd remembered from the catalog, painted white with scrolled sleigh ends and exquisite wood carving along the bottom.

"You can't cry," he said, coming to her side. "This is supposed to be a happy moment."

"It is. I am happy." She heard the trepidation in her own voice. The truth was that this was all happening at lightning speed, and even with her usually optimistic worldview, it was hard to not be overwhelmed by the weight of what was ahead. Motherhood was the great unknown and she was barreling toward it.

"This is a good thing, isn't it? A baby's gotta have somewhere to sleep."

"Of course. I'm just surprised, that's all. And things seem to be moving so fast. I'm starting to feel overwhelmed, just thinking about everything I have to do for the nursery and the holidays on the way. It's a lot to think about." She hated unloading on Andrew. Like he cared about all of her problems.

"I don't want you to worry. Just enjoy this moment, okay?"

"Okay." She turned and sought the comfort of his arms. It was such an appealing escape that she didn't question the repercussions of what this physical closeness meant. He didn't hesitate to wrap himself around her, pulling her close. He was so solid and firm, and she felt safe there, like nothing could ever hurt her or the baby.

He caressed her back slowly, bringing up feelings that went beyond comfort. She fought back her own desires to touch him, to have him touch her. They were all alone in this big house with nothing less than an entire weekend stretching out before them. It would be so easy to lean forward and kiss him, but she feared his response. Would he recoil? Push her away? Leave town? There was too much of a potential stigma standing between them—a widow and her husband's brother should not become physically involved. Even if she wanted him badly.

"Thank you so much for this. It's wonderful." She

didn't let go of him, resting her head on his chest and selfishly curling her fingers into his muscled back. "The fact that my brother helped you put it together really means so much to me. It makes the whole thing very special."

"I really like him a lot." He continued his lazy passes up and down the channel of her spine with his fingers. It was putting her into a trance, one where she was lulled into thinking everything would be okay. Even if she decided to act on her impulses.

"I'm so glad. He's a wonderful person. I don't know what I would've done without him over the years."

"He's great. But I think the real reason I like him is because he reminds me of you."

For a moment, Andrew's words hung in the air. At first, she thought that it was only natural that he would like her. Of course he did. She liked him, too. "That's sweet of you to say."

"It's the truth, Miranda. I know we've only been in the same house together for less than seven days, but it's been one of the best weeks in recent memory. That's all because of you."

"It's not just me," she said, finally lifting her head from his chest so she could look him in the eye. His face was painted with its usual serious expression, but she saw the vulnerability there, that he seemingly hid from other people. "You're half of this equation. You've cooked for me this week and been my companion. It might sound silly, but it's meant the world to me. I haven't been this happy in a while."

"Since before Johnathon passed away?"

Something about his statement struck a chord, and that made her stomach sink. Yes, she had happy memories of Johnathon, but she couldn't remember simply being happy on the days that were normal. There was always an air of discontent with Johnathon, a need to have more from life. Tara had once told Miranda that she'd felt like that the entire time she'd been married to Johnathon. Miranda hadn't thought much of it at the time, but now she got it, only because she'd seen a glimpse of what it was like to have more, even when there was no romance between her and Andrew.

"I don't think I could put a date on it," Miranda said, deciding that was enough information. "I only know that I'm happy right now."

A smile played at the corners of his tempting mouth. She wanted nothing more than to kiss him right now—or even better, have him kiss her. Have him show her that he wanted her. She wasn't sure he ever would. He might just be a fantasy right now. And perhaps that was for the best. Keep these crazy ideas of hers tucked up inside of her head.

"I'm so glad." He gripped her shoulders and pressed his lips to the top of her head. It felt like confirmation of the role in his life—sister-in-law or friend. "So, I wanted to tell you that I made a decision today while I was talking to your brother."

"Decision?"

"Yes. You'd mentioned Thanksgiving the day I moved in and Clay told me how much it means to you. Since things aren't quite wrapped up with Victor and Thanksgiving is next week, I just wanted to let you know that I'll be here for it. I'm happy to help with whatever you need."

Miranda was a lucky woman, and she needed to be grateful for the way things were. That meant she needed to stop making wishes about things that would never be. "Sounds perfect. I'm glad you decided to stay."

Five

Thanksgiving had never been a big deal in the Sterling household when Andrew was growing up. Their father had been injured at work when Johnathon and Andrew were young, which left their mom as the sole earner. Not a lot of money and a mother who was already pushing herself to the very limits of her abilities meant that big celebrations or big meals never took place. Often, Thanksgiving day meant burgers wrapped in paper from a drive-thru. Andrew couldn't blame it on anyone. It was simply a confluence of bad circumstances. And now he was the only one left on earth who recalled any of it. As far as he was concerned, it might be time to make new memories, starting with today.

Andrew and Miranda had spent most of the night before baking pies and planning out the Thanksgiving menu. Like all time he spent with her in that house, it brought him nothing less than pure happiness. They had forged a bond, especially since the day he put the crib together with Clay's help. But Andrew was haunted a bit by the scene in the nursery after the big reveal. Having Miranda in his arms brought too many good feelings that he wasn't sure he deserved. He'd wanted to give in to the cues his body was sending during those quiet moments, the ones that said he should cup her jaw and kiss her. That he should sweep her into his arms, carry her off to the bedroom and make love to her.

What had stopped him? The overwhelming presence of his brother and the sense that he wasn't entitled to someone as lovely and sweet as Miranda. So he'd kissed her on the head, made a promise to stay for Thanksgiving and taken thoughts of her to bed that night. He wasn't proud of what had gone through his mind while he imagined her asleep right down the hall…the way he'd fantasized about touching her beautiful body and bringing her to her peak again and again. Even now, those thoughts were pervasive. They followed him wherever he went.

"I think we're all set," Miranda said, adjusting one of the place settings at the table in her dining room.

"Absolutely. It's beautiful," Andrew said. "Just like everything you do." *Just like you, period.*

The doorbell rang and Miranda jumped. "Somebody's here." She practically squealed like a little girl on Christmas morning. Her enthusiasm was infectious as she traipsed off down the hall and Andrew followed. "If Grant and Tara aren't being nice, just ignore them," she said before flinging open the door.

Fortunately for Andrew, it was Astrid, Clay and his daughter, Delia.

"Aunt Miranda!" the little girl exclaimed, then flattened herself against Miranda's legs, wrapping her arms around her.

Miranda leaned down and kissed Delia on top of the head. "Hi, sweetie. Happy Thanksgiving."

Clay handed Andrew a bottle of wine. "Andrew, I'd like you to meet Astrid."

A former model, Astrid was just as stunning as the photographs Andrew had seen. One thing was indisputable—Johnathon had been a very lucky man. "It's so nice to meet you, Andrew. It feels strange that you were once my brother-in-law, but we never met."

Of the many things that were going to be awkward today, that detail might be pretty high on the list. "Better late than never, right?"

Clay slid Andrew a look of solidarity. He and Andrew had discussed the contentious nature of Andrew's relationship with Johnathon. Clay seemed to understand that it had been messy and complicated.

"Come on, everyone. Let me make some drinks," Andrew said, waving everyone into the great room.

Just as the five of them arrived, the doorbell rang again.

"I'll get it," Miranda said, flitting off for the front door.

Andrew went to work, pouring glasses of wine for Clay and Astrid, and making a Shirley Temple for Delia.

"It's so fancy with a cherry in it." Delia eagerly sucked on the straw.

"Not too fast," Clay offered. "We don't need you bouncing off the walls."

Delia rolled her eyes. "Okay, Daddy."

"Look who's here," Miranda said, entering the room with Tara and Grant in her wake.

Tara went to hug Astrid while Grant shook Clay's hand. Andrew felt like the odd man out here, and it was no surprise. The last time he'd seen Grant and Tara, it had been at a party in downtown San Diego a few weeks after Johnathon's death. That had been Andrew's first attempt to stop the plan to sabotage Sterling Enterprises. It was also when Grant and Tara confronted him about the fact that he hadn't been to the funeral. That ultimately led to Andrew's visit to see Miranda and apologize. If he had to admit it, it was also when his fascination with Miranda had started. But he would keep that to himself forever.

"Andrew," Grant said. He offered his hand, but everything in his tone was clipped and curt.

"Grant," Andrew countered. "Nice to see you."

The look on Tara's face said she wasn't really buying it. "I see you decided to stay for Thanksgiving," she said. The subtext, of course, was that Andrew had no business being there.

"Miranda asked me to stay. It's her first Thanksgiving without Johnathon."

"And are you thinking you're a substitute?" Tara asked.

Andrew's stomach lurched. He so greatly disliked the suggestion. "No. I'm not."

Thankfully, Miranda appeared, which made both Tara and Grant relax. Apparently, they were saving their contention for only him. "Andrew, it's about time to take the turkey out of the oven."

He consulted his watch. "So it is."

"I'll come with you," Miranda said.

Andrew had never looked more forward to a trip to the kitchen. At least he and Miranda could be alone. "Tara and Grant aren't happy I'm here," he said as he read the temperature readout on the digital thermometer. He grabbed the oven mitts and turned off the oven, then opened the door. The aroma of roast turkey filled the room, reminding him of what he was really here for—not to please Tara and Grant, but to make Miranda happy.

"I hope you know that I don't care what they think," Miranda said as she got out the carving knife and large cutting board.

"But I think you *do* care. You're so thoughtful. You care about everyone."

"Not at the sake of someone else's feelings." She turned to Andrew and grasped his forearm. "You're here because I want you here. This is one of my most favorite days of the year and I can't imagine it without you right now, okay? So let's just get a few glasses of wine into Grant and Tara, sit down to a fabulous meal, and try to forget everything else."

She had such a way of calming him. It was incredible. "Sounds perfect." He leaned forward and kissed her on the temple. It was only a peck, but how he wished he could have lingered longer with his lips. He wanted a touch that was more than fleeting, a whiff of her intoxicating fragrance that lasted longer than a heartbeat. Those unfulfilled desires left a hot ache in the center of his chest that echoed the regret he felt at not being able to clutch her nape, raise her chin, and deliver a real kiss.

The pair were soon joined by Astrid, who helped them ferry dishes of decadent mashed potatoes, green beans with crispy shallots, and herb stuffing to the sideboard in the dining room. Buttery dinner rolls, sweet potato casserole, turkey and gravy soon followed. It was quite a production, but you never would have known it was any work at all judging by Miranda's sunny mood. Andrew had suggested days ago that she consider hiring some help for the occa-

sion, but she'd been strictly opposed to the idea. She
wanted this to be about family.

As they sat down to the table, with Miranda at
the head of the table and Clay at the opposite end,
Andrew was struck by two things. First, it was sad
that this was such an unfamiliar setting for him. He'd
seen it in movies and, yes, he'd been to a few fancy
Thanksgiving celebrations, but nothing as family-
oriented as this. Second, he still felt like the inter-
loper. Miranda may have said she wanted him here,
but Johnathon's absence was omnipresent. It was all
around them. And the logical deduction from that
fact was that if Johnathon had still been alive, Andrew wouldn't have been sitting at this table at all.

The meal was wonderful, and everyone seemed to
enjoy themselves, even Tara and Grant. Perhaps Miranda had been right. Maybe they'd just needed some
wine to smooth away their rougher edges. After dessert, which was an array of pies—pumpkin, pecan,
and apple—Clay and Astrid went to play with Delia
in the backyard, leaving Andrew and Miranda with
Tara and Grant.

"So, Andrew, how long do you think you'll be
staying?" Tara asked.

"As long as he wants," Miranda quickly answered.
"It's great to have someone here at the house with
me."

"But the plan is to go back to Seattle, right? After

you sort things out with the problem you created?" Grant asked.

"Yes. I have made Victor an offer to stop with what he's doing. I'm just not sure he's received it. That's been the hard part. Getting a hold of him."

Grant nodded but seemed entirely unconvinced. "You know what's interesting?"

"What?" Andrew replied, sensing something bad was about to be lobbed in his direction.

"Things at Sterling have been remarkably quieter since you arrived. We've had zero problems." Grant sat back in his chair and crossed his legs.

"Maybe that means Victor is backing off," Miranda said.

Tara shook her head. "Or maybe it means that there is no Victor."

Andrew drew a deep cleansing breath through his nose. He would not lose his cool. He deserved this. He'd created the problem in the first place and he was going to have to fix his own mess. "If I could prove to you that he exists, I would. But for the time being, you're just going to have to take me at my word."

Miranda's heart was in her throat as she listened to the back-and-forth between Andrew, Grant and Tara. He explained that Victor was a man who did as much of his work as he could off the books, using offshore accounts and holding companies. Victor liked being invisible and that would make him much harder to stop.

It all sounded unreal to Miranda, but she had faith in Andrew. Her only disappointment was how much she hated the acrimony, especially on a holiday that she'd so looked forward to. Perhaps it was best if this all came out now so it could finally be gone and she could stop thinking about it. If that could be her reward, she felt a need to play a bigger role in putting it all to an end.

"I believe Andrew. One hundred percent. There's no doubt in my mind." Miranda sat a little straighter, as if she could convey her conviction with her body language.

Andrew turned to her, his eyes full of surprise, when really she'd expected him to be feeling hurt. Tara and Grant had said some terrible things. "Thank you. I appreciate your confidence in me."

"Miranda, can you and I talk in the other room?" Tara asked, getting up from her chair.

Miranda wasn't about to split this up until it was settled. "Whatever you have to say to me, you can say in front of Andrew. I don't see any reason to go in the other room."

Tara shot her a look that suggested Miranda was crazy. "I really think it would be good if we had some privacy."

Miranda felt her anger growing by the minute.

"No. Tell me now. Whatever horrible thing you have to say, just come out with it."

"Guys, can we cool down for a minute here?" Andrew asked. "Miranda has been looking forward to today for a very long time. She worked her butt off and I don't think it's fair that we're robbing her of this moment."

Good God, he was such a sweet and thoughtful man. If Tara and Grant couldn't see that, they weren't paying attention. "Thank you, Andrew. I appreciate that."

"Neither of us is trying to ruin Thanksgiving," Grant said. "But, Miranda, I would be remiss in my role as Johnathon's best friend if I didn't say that I think Andrew is taking advantage of you." He turned to Andrew. "I don't know what your endgame is here, but none of this adds up. I don't know Victor, and I knew all of Johnathon's business deals. I knew everyone he dealt with. And more than anything, I have a deep familiarity with everything that went bad at Sterling Enterprises. That's why I don't believe there's a Victor. I think you're using it as a front to hide the things you did, or at the very least, as an excuse to get out of apologizing for trying to kneecap your brother's business."

"You're wrong," Andrew said. "I've already apologized. Victor is very real and it's only a matter of time until he does something to hurt Sterling. That's why I'm here. To stop that from happening. So I don't know what else to tell you, but you're wrong."

"That's not good enough," Tara said. "I want to know what's really going on here. Are you cozying up to Miranda because you're hoping you can get your hooks into Sterling Enterprises that way?"

Andrew pushed back from the table and tossed his napkin onto his plate. "That's enough. I'll excuse myself now." He turned to Miranda, nearly shaking with rage. "I'll get to work on the kitchen. I don't want the rest of your evening to be ruined by having to listen to this." He walked out of the room with determined strides.

Miranda's heart was currently residing in her stomach. How had everything gone so wrong? "What the hell, you two? Did you seriously just blow up my Thanksgiving dinner?"

Tara reached for Miranda's hand, but Miranda wasn't about to play at that game and she yanked it back into her lap. "Miranda. I'm sorry, but I just don't understand what he's getting out of this whole equation. Living in your house, chasing around some guy who we're pretty sure doesn't exist. I don't think the company is in trouble anymore. I believe that he put a stop to his plan, and I suppose he deserves credit for that, but otherwise, I think he's lying to you."

Miranda did her best to compose herself, but she could feel her blood about to boil. Why couldn't Tara and Grant take off their blinders about Andrew and accept that she was enjoying having him in her life? "Look. Here's the deal. I believe him. I believe him with every bone in my body. And you have to understand that he's not only my connection to Johnathon, he's the baby's connection, as well. If you can't imagine why that might be important to me right now, then I don't know what to say." She nearly gasped for breath when she finished. It had come out as a long string of words, but at least it had come from the heart.

Tara's head dropped to one side. "Miranda. Grant and I want the best for you. We're trying to protect you. All we know is that if Johnathon knew what was going on right now, he'd go through the roof. That's why we had to say something. We couldn't let it go."

"You can guess all you want about how Johnathon would've reacted to this, but the reality is that he isn't here right now. The rest of us are. And if we can't find a way to come together, this baby isn't going to have a family."

"Are you including Andrew in that?" Grant asked.

"Yes. I am."

For a moment, no one said a peep, and Miranda was thankful for the silence, but what she really wanted was for everyone to go home so she and Andrew could be alone and she could tell him how deeply sorry she was that this had happened. She was disappointed that her Thanksgiving had been ruined, but much more than that, she hated that he had been so hurt in the process.

"I'm going to help Andrew in the kitchen." Miranda rose from the table and collected a few plates.

"Here. Let me help," Tara said, getting up from her chair.

"No. Please. Don't," Miranda said. "I can do it. If you want to spend time with Clay and Astrid, feel free. But otherwise, it's probably best if you go home."

Grant's face fell. "I don't want to leave knowing that you're so upset."

Miranda shrugged. "I'll get over it. I still love you both. But it's best for me right now if you just go." With that, she made her exit from the dining room. When she arrived in the kitchen, she spotted Andrew and Clay talking. They were smiling. Laughing even. This was what she'd hoped for today. Family and togetherness. She'd take this tiny moment and tuck it away in her head for later. The holiday wasn't a total loss.

"Everything okay in there?" Clay asked.

"Tara and Grant are leaving. They were being a pain in my butt." Miranda placed the stack of plates on the counter, then began filling the sink with hot water.

Clay came up to her. "I'm sorry. Honestly, I think the stress of planning their wedding is getting to them. I think they've been fighting about it. Grant has a huge family and they're all coming. I think Tara thought they wouldn't show up and she could have something supersmall."

Tara and Grant were getting married right before Christmas. If that was the problem, at least it would eventually go away. It still didn't make Miranda feel any better. "Maybe."

Astrid and Delia came in through the French doors just off the kitchen. "Are we ready?" Astrid asked. "I'm exhausted from running around the backyard."

Clay grinned wide, his expression so full of love it was hard for Miranda to wrap her head around it. Her brother had found happiness. Not everything was terrible.

"Speaking of weddings," Miranda said. "Have you two thought about setting a date?"

Clay and Astrid looked at each other. "We haven't. We're too busy having fun," Astrid said. "We'll worry about that later."

How Miranda loved that attitude. Taking the good in the moment and not stressing about the rest.

"Thanks for hosting," Clay said, offering Miranda a hug.

"Thank you so much for coming." She stepped out of her brother's embrace and wrapped her arms around Delia and Astrid, who were standing together. She watched as Andrew bid his farewell. There was already a genuine warmth between Clay and Andrew. That had to count for something. Andrew wasn't a bad guy. He simply wasn't.

The happy little family unit of Clay, Astrid and Delia made their departure, leaving Miranda and Andrew all alone with a messy kitchen.

"I'm officially regretting my choice to not bring in any help." Miranda swished dish soap in the sink full of hot water.

"I'm sorry," Andrew said, stepping closer to her and trying to make eye contact.

"Don't be. It was your suggestion. I was the dummy who didn't listen."

He shook his head and laughed softly. "That's not what I'm talking about. I'm talking about the scene with Grant and Tara. That wouldn't have happened if I hadn't been here."

Miranda held up her finger. "No. Don't say that. It's their problem, not yours."

He pursed his lips and leaned against the counter. "I heard what you said after I left. I went back to grab some dishes and I overheard. I want you to know that I appreciate everything you said on my behalf. You shouldn't have to stick up for me."

"I had to say something. They were in the wrong. I couldn't let it go." Even with the heavy subject of their conversation, Miranda did feel a weight lifting. It was just her and Andrew now. She didn't need to worry about everyone else and their agendas.

"It meant a lot to me. Truly. Everything today

did." Andrew reached for Miranda's hand. "The last two weeks have been some of the best of my whole life. I'm sure that sounds stupid, but it's the truth."

Her heart fluttered when he squeezed her fingers, making her feel equal parts excited and foolish. "It's not stupid. I feel the same way. I love having you here." She scanned his face for some sign of what he meant by holding on to her hand so tightly, but then he licked his lower lip and her knees nearly buckled. His mouth was way too gorgeous. His shoulders were too broad and his hair too touchable. She wanted nothing more than to thread her fingers through it, curl her fingers into his scalp and wrap her leg around his hip.

Before she knew what was happening, Andrew locked his gaze on her. There was an actual jolt to her system—a connection made. They drifted closer, the space between them slowly disappearing and time becoming elastic. Miranda struggled to keep up. Logic told her to look away, but she couldn't. It felt like the key to tomorrow was in his eyes and she had to find it.

His hand went to her jaw, his fingertips giving the lightest imaginable touch against her neck. "I'm afraid I'm going to make a mistake, Miranda."

Her heart was beating so fast it was either going to burst or give out. "What do you mean?" She was desperate for the answer, but it was a terrifying prospect. If he pulled away from her, it would take a long time to recover. She'd spent too much time over the last few months trying to get past unwelcome truths. Today, she wanted her reality to have at least a sliver of good news.

"I want to kiss you. But I worry that it's wrong." His warm palm rested on her jaw, his heat pouring into her.

Her mind scrambled for an elegant answer, but she didn't have a clever or witty reply. She was too relieved that they'd both been thinking the exact same thing. She didn't know how long he'd felt this way, but time didn't matter right now. The only thing she cared about was hurrying down this path he'd just set them on. "Maybe you should just try it and see how right it feels."

Six

The air in the kitchen was charged with anticipation.

"If I kiss you, Miranda, there's no going back." Andrew dropped his chin, working his way into Miranda's psyche with an intense flash of his eyes. His one free hand went to the other side of her face.

Miranda was all too aware of her breaths, her galloping heartbeat, the rotating sway of her body in his presence. This wasn't that different from the moment up in the baby's nursery, when she'd so desperately wanted him to touch her. Everywhere. "I don't see the point in going back, Andrew. I'm only interested in moving forward." Why wasn't he kissing her? Was he waiting for her to do it? She wished she'd come up with a sexier reply, but words seemed so useless now. She was too busy managing urges, like the one that said she'd finally be happy if he wasn't wearing that shirt. Or those pants.

"I need to be sure." He leaned even closer and kissed her cheek. "Absolutely positive that this is what you want."

If he didn't kiss her for real, she was about to explode. She popped up onto her toes, gripping his shoulders to steady herself. "I'm positive."

She closed her eyes and went for it—her lips met his in a kiss that made it feel like she was floating. There was only the slightest hesitation before his tongue slipped along her lower lip. Every atom in her body celebrated in a chorus of delight and relief. She shifted her forearms up onto his shoulders, dug her fingers into the back of his thick hair. His lips—soft and warm and wet—became more eager, seeking her jaw and neck. His arms wound tightly around her, pulling her against him, nearly lifting her off her toes.

His hand snaked under the back of her sweater, confirming what she'd been so unsure of before—he wanted her. He wanted clothes to come off as badly as she did. His fingers fumbled with her bra clasp, which was more than a little adorable. Andrew was always so sure of himself. It made him so human. And it made her feel ever so slightly closer to him.

"Here. Let me," she muttered. Now flat-footed, she lifted her sweater over her head, then clutched it to her chest. She could admit to being unsure of what he would say when he saw her pregnant form.

"Are you hiding from me?" he asked.

"No. I mean, yes. Maybe a little. Have you ever had to have sex with a pregnant woman?"

"Had to? I want to." He plucked the sweater from her hands and placed it on the kitchen counter. Leaning closer, he hooked his finger under one of the straps of her white silk bra, then popped it off her shoulder. "Everything about your body is luscious and beautiful. I can't wait to see every inch."

His words didn't merely prompt a wild wave of goose bumps—they were about to become a permanent memory, etched in her mind. She bit down on her lip. If this was going to happen, it would be good. She reached behind her and unhooked her bra, but left it for him to take it off.

"Keep going." He kissed the curve of her neck, the most sensitive spot, the one that made her arch her back and nearly call out from the pleasure.

She took his direction and slipped the garment forward from her shoulders. He helped by pulling it down the length of her arms. His vision sank lower and her heart picked up in anticipation. Gripping her rib cage with both hands, his thumbs caressed the tender underside of her breasts as he lowered his head and gave one nipple a gentle lick.

The gasp that rose from the depths of her throat sounded like weeks of frustration being cut loose.

She dropped her chin to her chest when he did it again. She loved watching him admire her this way, knowing that she turned him on. "I want you, Andrew. Now."

"Upstairs," he answered.

Before she could take a single step, she was off her feet and in his arms, feeling like she weighed nothing at all. Considering her pregnant state, it was an amazing feeling. He marched down the hall and up the stairs as she clung to his neck, desperate to kiss him again.

"Your bedroom or mine?" he asked. The weight of the question was impossible to ignore. Her bedroom was where she'd slept with Johnathon.

It was too much to think about right now, so she gave the simplest answer. "Yours. It's closer."

He grinned. "I like the way you think."

They reached their destination, his beautifully appointed room. He set her down gently on the king-size bed, smiling again. He stood back and began unbuttoning his shirt. The soft evening light showed off the incredible contours and definition of his chest and abs. He had a lovely patch of dark hair in the center and a most enticing narrow trail extending from his belly button that disappeared behind the waistband of his pants. His shoulders were even better than she could've imagined. Not even a well-tailored suit coat did them justice. They were square and broad. They begged for her touch.

He stepped closer to the bed, and she sat up, flattening her hands against his firm chest, his skin warming her palms and fingers. With her arms raised, he cupped her breasts, making her drop back her head for a moment. It felt so good that it made her head swim. She forced herself to straighten, only because she was desperate to have his mouth on hers again. As if she'd spoken her desire, he leaned down and gave her a long, deep kiss. The sort of kiss that made a woman lose her mind.

She would've been lying if she'd said she wasn't eager to see the rest of him. She unzipped his pants and pushed them to the floor, then dipped her fingers beneath the waistband of his black boxer briefs, tugging them down his trim hips. He kissed her again, and she wrapped her fingers around his erection, loving the deep moan that went straight from his mouth to hers.

He gently pushed on her shoulder, urging her to lie back, then he kissed the bare mound of her stomach. He was so tender and sweet, it took her breath away. She watched as he unbuttoned her trousers and wiggled them down the length of her legs. His eyes roved all over her body, full of admiration that made her heart swell. Everything between her legs was begging for his touch. Her whole body froze with the anticipation.

He tugged down her panties, casting his dark eyes up toward hers as his fingers met her center. She couldn't let go of her grip on his head as he artfully rocked his hand back and forth. It felt impossibly good to be at his mercy. To be wanted and desired the way she had been thinking of him so often over the last few weeks. Their gazes connected, and it was as if she saw more of him, parts that he expended so much energy to hide. The parts of him that were hurt.

The pressure was building, the peak upon her, but she wanted more. She wanted a deeper connection. She needed him. Inside her. "Please make love to me, Andrew," she said. She disbelieved the words as soon as they left her lips. This was such a crazy, inexplicable situation they were in, and yet it was the only thing that seemed right.

He pressed more soft kisses against her stomach. "Do you want me to use a condom?"

She giggled a bit. "You do know I'm pregnant."

"And I want to be sure you know that I'm clean. I haven't been with anyone in a very long time."

She loved that he showed such utter care and concern, but she was confounded by what he'd said. He was so damn handsome and sexy. It seemed improbable that he didn't have women vying for him constantly. Perhaps that was a topic for another time, when she didn't have such urgent needs. "We're good then."

He stretched out next to her, a truly magnificent male specimen, strong and muscled, but nimble and lean. He dropped back his head when she coiled her fingers around him and stroked his length. She could hardly believe how much tension his body was holding. When their eyes connected, he looked as if he wanted to consume her, which was a good thing. It was exactly what she wanted.

"Is it better for you and the baby if you're on top or the bottom?" he asked.

She hadn't thought about this. She'd never had to worry about her pregnant belly before, but it was still a very modest pooch. It wouldn't get in the way. "I want to be on the bottom this time. I want to feel you weigh me down."

"And that's okay with the baby?"

"Right now? Yes. She's the size of a tennis ball."

Andrew positioned himself between her legs and she arched her back to meet him, welcoming him as he sank into her. He took things slow and careful, with a patience she relished. Her mind swam as their bodies met and she began to experience each delightful physical sensation. She'd hadn't taken the time to let her fantasies about Andrew venture this far, but nothing could have prepared her for how good he felt.

He rolled his hips when his body met hers. It built the pressure at her apex quickly, her breaths coming faster now. Her hands roamed over the muscled landscape of his back, trailing down to his spectacular backside. His kisses were deep and passionate, matching the steady and satisfying rock of their bodies. She wrapped her legs around him, wanting him closer. Deeper.

She placed her hands on the side of his face, keeping his lips to hers. She wanted to be connected with him when she came apart at the seams. She kept her mind focused on the here and now, waiting only for the bliss awaiting her, without a worry in the world.

Miranda was close—he could feel it. He sensed it in every sexy movement of her body. He was fighting off his own orgasm, which was a near impossible task. Concentrating on her breaths and the grip of her hands on the side of his face was the only way to do it. They were a beautiful distraction from the pressure coiling tight in his belly.

Her breathing was ragged now. Every pleasurable sound she made was a boost to his ego, but he wasn't prepared for the moment when she called his name, clutching his back and digging her nails into his back. The pain was such a delicious counterpoint to the pleasure as she tensed around him, her body holding on to his as if she'd never let go.

Tension had him wrapped up so tight that rational thought was gone. Pure instinct took over as a smile spread across her face and he took a few final strokes. The pressure finally relented and his body gave in to the pleasure. It rocketed through him, setting every nerve ending on fire.

He was quick to roll to his side, not wanting to put

any unnecessary weight on the baby. Miranda rolled to her side and curled into him, resting her head in the crook of his armpit. He struggled to catch his breath, but part of him never wanted that to happen. He knew that as soon as his heart rate returned to normal, logical and difficult thoughts would walk right into his brain.

"That was amazing." She tangled her fingers in his chest hair, then craned her neck to kiss him.

Their lips met and there was more to it now than there had been before. He should've known he would feel this way now that the ice had been broken between them. He wanted her even more than he had several hours ago. He feared that he would never get enough.

"You're the amazing one, Miranda. Truly."

She laughed quietly and kissed his chest. "You're spoiling me."

"There's no such thing. You deserve to be spoiled. Rotten. Absolutely showered with affection and praise and expensive jewelry. Real estate. Yachts."

She popped up onto her elbow and looked him square in the face. "I never asked for a boat."

Now it was his turn to laugh. "My point was that I'll give you whatever you want." As soon as the words had left his lips and he'd had a second to absorb the ramifications, he worried that he'd gone too far. But just as quick, he decided that he'd wasted way too much time worrying about the things he'd done. There was nothing wrong with that statement. It had been uttered in the moment and it had come from the heart. He meant it. Every last word.

"I don't need much," she answered. "I really don't."

"Then tell me. Tell me what you want."

She was quiet for a moment and the stillness seemed to take over the room. He would've paid anything to have a glimpse inside her head, to know her innermost thoughts. He worried that she might not share what was truly there.

"I want life to be good and normal. I want to be happy." She settled her head back on his shoulder. "I know that sounds stupid and boring, but it's the truth."

He rubbed her lower back with his hand, relishing the velvety touch of her skin. "It's not boring. I think it's beautiful in its simplicity. Plus, those are things you can't buy. I have to appreciate that."

"They also feel like the hardest things to come by."

We could be happy. The thought flew into his consciousness lightning-fast. He knew from experience that those instantaneous ideas that crop up in one's head were the most real. The ones that came from the heart. "Also the things worth fighting for, right?"

She nodded silently. "Can I tell you something? Something that I'm not very proud of?"

"A confession?"

"Yes. I suppose."

"I find it hard to believe that you have a single thing to be ashamed of or to confess."

She draped her hand across his belly and pulled him a little closer. "It's not something I did so much as it's something I thought. That day when we were in the nursery. After you surprised me with the crib. When I said that I was happy you were here."

He couldn't imagine what she was about to say, and part of him was scared to know, but he also didn't have it in his heart to tell her no. "Tell me, Miranda. I won't judge you."

She let go of a heavy breath. "It occurred to me then that I might not have been truly happy when I was with Johnathon."

This wasn't exactly a topic he was eager to explore, but he did want to know what she meant by that. "Were there problems?"

"No. There weren't. In fact, we were still sort of in that honeymoon phase, where everything seems easy. Do you know what I mean?"

"Actually, I don't. I've never been married." He'd come close once, but that wasn't something he cared to reveal right now.

"It's not even about marriage. It's just that giddy stage where the other person can do no wrong. But I don't know that we had any truly deep feelings between us. Everything with Johnathon was a whirlwind. Dating, our engagement, the wedding. It all happened so fast and I wonder if I just got carried away with it."

Andrew had heard women tell similar tales of being swept off their feet by Johnathon. It wasn't Andrew's style. It never had been. He wanted something deeper. He always had. "Do you think you're feeling this way because you found out that he cheated on you?"

"Maybe." She drummed her fingers on his chest, bringing every nerve ending in his body back to life. "I guess that's probably it. You're so smart."

He'd just slept with his brother's widow. He wasn't sure that applied to him right now. "I don't know about that, but thank you." He wanted to set them back on a happier course of conversation, one that hopefully didn't include Johnathon. "Are you sure you don't want to add anything to your list of what you want? Not a diamond necklace or a fancy car?"

"Honestly? No. But I'm a little afraid to tell you what I really want."

He reared back his head and looked down at her. He loved seeing her lovely face peering up at him. "Don't be afraid. Just tell me."

"I want to decorate for Christmas tomorrow."

"You're kidding me."

She shook her head. "Nope. I love the holidays, Thanksgiving was a semidisaster, and as far as I'm concerned, the Christmas season starts at midnight tonight. I don't want to waste a single minute not celebrating, and for me, that means transforming the house into a winter wonderland."

"In Southern California."

"Yep."

He grinned and pulled her closer. "You got it. We can decorate all day if you want."

"Great. But now you have to tell me what you want."

Did it really need saying? He supposed it did. "What I really want tonight is you."

Seven

In the light of day, waking up in Andrew's room, Miranda's first thoughts were decidedly more conflicted than any she'd had the night before. Her evening with Andrew had been both unexpected and incredible. In fact, it had been so amazing that guilt was threatening to eat away at the otherwise pleasant state she was in. She wouldn't allow the bad feelings to swallow her whole, but they were there, circling above her head and threatening to swoop in.

Andrew wasn't there with her in bed, but that was no big surprise. He didn't seem to sleep much. He certainly hadn't last night. In fact, he'd worn her out. But she'd needed that level of pure physical exhaustion. It had cleared her head after a difficult and crazy day. She sat up in his bed and let her feet dangle over the edge. Maybe it was the afterglow, but making love with Andrew had been transformative. She felt different this morning. More alive.

She tiptoed into her bedroom and grabbed a short, sexy nightgown, plus her silk robe. Taking a minute in her bathroom, she brushed her teeth, tamed her hair and spritzed on a bit of perfume. She wanted to look and smell good for Andrew. She wanted him to want her, like he had last night. A taste of him simply wasn't enough.

When she walked back through her bedroom to the hall, something stopped her—the picture of her and Johnathon on her wedding day, perched on top of her dresser. The gravity of what they'd done hit her. It was a little more than three months since Johnathon had died. Had she given herself enough time to grieve? How long was that supposed to be, anyway? She wasn't sure of the timeline, but she had to think it was longer than that. What would people say? Especially if they found out that the person she'd become tangled up with was Andrew, her dead husband's brother?

Nothing about this was fair. She'd endured more pain than she'd thought possible when she lost her husband, but despite that, she was still here, with a beating heart and desperate to give and receive love. Andrew was a kind and compassionate man. He was sexy and strong. He was also forever tied to someone she'd loved immensely. Of course she was going to have strong feelings for him. That part was baked into the mix. What harm was there in them expressing affection for each other?

None, she decided. What had happened last night had not hurt a single person. And she truly failed to see why it was of any concern to anyone in the first place. She deserved a sliver of happiness just as much as the next person. So did Andrew. Anyone else's preconceived notions about right or wrong in this situation were not her problem. No one else knew her soul, her innermost thoughts or the realities of her life. No one else knew what could make her happy.

It wasn't easy, but she forced herself to push past the moment, look beyond the photograph, and walk out the door and into the hall. With every step, she felt more determined. Meanwhile, the pleasant aroma of fresh coffee teased her nose. That brought a smile to her face and a flush of heat to her cheeks in anticipation of seeing Andrew. She'd been limiting herself to one cup a day since she learned she was pregnant, but she'd had a hard time giving up that little bit of caffeine. How nice it was to have someone else brew a pot, just as Andrew had done every morning since he'd moved in. It was a surprising bright spot in her day. Even when he'd come on a mission that was decidedly not sunny, he'd brought happiness into her home.

When she stepped into the kitchen, she was

greeted by a breathtaking sight—Andrew in pajama pants and no shirt, busy cooking. She'd known last night that she was a lucky woman, but this morning was proving the theory again. The pj's were a dark navy plaid with a drawstring he hadn't bothered to tie, leaving the enticing contours of his hips and lower abs on full display.

"Good morning," she said, drifting into him, drawn to his bare chest the way a duck wants to be in the water.

"Good morning to you." Andrew pulled her into his arms and wrapped her up tight, kissing the top of her head again and again.

She closed her eyes and soaked up his touch. She could get used to this, but that might not be wise. Andrew had been clear—he planned to return to Seattle as soon as the situation with Victor was resolved. Miranda couldn't leave San Diego. Her ties here—to her brother, niece and Astrid, and even to Grant, Tara and Sterling Enterprises—ran deep. For now, she couldn't bring herself to think about that. She would enjoy her time with Andrew and deal with life and logistics later.

Reluctantly, she opened her eyes and spotted the roasting pan from yesterday. "Oh, my God. We completely forgot to clean the kitchen last night."

He started laughing and released her from his warm embrace. "We were pretty distracted, weren't we?"

She surveyed the kitchen, which was nearly spotless. "How long have you been up?"

"Since seven."

A quick glance at the clock said that it was 9:15 a.m. She helped herself to a cup of coffee, adding a splash of cream and a spoonful of raw sugar. "I'm so sorry. Why didn't you wake me?"

He cast her a disapproving look that suggested she needed to have her head examined. "Are you kidding me? Nobody wakes a pregnant woman. It's like poking a bear."

She disliked the comparison to a large, hairy mammal, but he wasn't far off base. "You're my guest. You shouldn't have to clean up such a big mess in the kitchen. Especially when you did half of the cooking yesterday."

He arched both eyebrows at her and picked up a dish from the sink, wiping it dry with a towel. "I think I moved beyond being a guest last night. At least I hope I did."

She felt like a heel. "That's not what I mean. I'm sorry. You're definitely far more than a guest. Really, I'm so sorry."

"Don't be. We're both in unfamiliar territory right now." He put the plate in the cabinet, then grabbed his mug from the counter and took a sip. His observation was spot-on, but as she thought about it, she took the chance to admire a few of his appealing features, like his slightly messy bed head and the flex of his forearm as he held the coffee to his lips. Even the questioning look in his eyes was beguiling, and that did nothing but fill her with doubt.

"You aren't wrong." Their journey from strangers to brother-in-law and sister-in-law, to friends, housemates and now lovers was not a typical trajectory.

"How are you feeling about things?" he asked. "I'm not the type to push heavy conversations, but I think we need to recognize that our situation is not the norm. Not even close. There are a lot of complicated feelings involved and as near as I can tell, there aren't any rules for this. That could be good, but it could also be bad."

His admission, although dismal at first glance, brought an overwhelming sense of relief. So she hadn't overreacted upstairs when she'd seen the photo of Johnathon and her. The many thoughts that had gone through her mind, all clashing with each other, were understandable. "I'd be lying if I said that I didn't feel conflicted."

"Good."

"Good?"

"Yes. I think it's good." The kitchen timer went off and Andrew sprang into action, grabbing an oven mitt and pulling a pie tin out of the oven.

Yet another amazing smell hit her nose—bacon and cheese. "You made quiche?"

He shrugged and set the pan on the cooktop. "I cook when I'm stressed. It helps me think."

Now she was starting to understand what he meant by "good." "So it's weighing on you, too."

"Of course it is. We crossed a line last night. Or at least I did."

"No. We both did. They're just different lines."

He drew in a breath, pursing his lips and seeming deep in thought. "I have to wonder how I'd be feeling right now if we hadn't given in to temptation."

Was he regretting their choice? Because as much as she felt at odds with her own moral compass, she refused to look at last night and express remorse. She'd needed more than the physical release—she'd craved his touch and tenderness. She'd needed to feel less like a vessel for a baby and more like a woman. Plus, she couldn't deny that her attraction to Andrew had grown so much over the last few weeks as they'd become closer and closer with each passing day. "I think I'd be feeling frustrated."

He nodded in agreement and reached for her hand, pulling her close until they were standing toe-to-toe. That one gesture meant the world to her right now. It was a lifeline. She'd been feeling adrift for the last few minutes as he grappled with the ramifications of the fact that they'd made love. "You're right. I'd be feeling the same way. My problem is that I've been struggling with my attraction to you since the day we met. And that was definitely not the right time to be feeling that way. In fact, it was absolutely wrong."

"You can't help the way you feel, Andrew."

"But I have to wonder if that's maybe the real reason I came back to San Diego. I probably could've dealt with Victor from Seattle. I'm worried that part of me wanted a chance with you. And that's not right. The guilt of that is squarely on my shoulders this morning."

She sighed, looking up into his handsome face. Again, she felt like she could see shades of his past in his eyes. His history. The pain. "You came here with good intentions. And you've been nothing but wonderful to me. I've needed you this whole time and you haven't hesitated to help."

"That still doesn't lighten the load on my conscience."

"Then what will?"

"Honestly? I don't know. It's too wrapped up in my feelings about my brother and how everything went wrong between us. It makes me sad just to think about all the time we wasted being at each other's throats and knowing that I can't make any of it right. It's too late."

"From everything you've said, it was both of you. You can't take all of the responsibility."

"I know. But I do. I'm here. He isn't." He shook his head and looked off in the distance for a moment, his forehead crinkling with worry. She hated seeing the physical manifestation of this burden. "I think they call that survivor's guilt. I probably need a therapist."

"Well, I'm no psychiatrist, but I'm a good listener.

We have the whole day ahead of us, and the weekend beyond that. If you feel like sharing, I'm all ears."

"While we decorate, right?"

She scrunched up her nose, hoping he wouldn't change his mind. She'd been looking forward to this since they'd talked about it in bed. "If that's okay. It's just one of my absolute favorite things in the whole world. When I was a kid, a big fancy Christmas was the one thing I always wanted, but never got. Now that I'm an adult, I don't miss the chance to get everything I couldn't have then."

"Totally understandable." He kissed her tenderly on the cheek. "It all sounds good to me."

Andrew couldn't help but question what he was doing, or more specifically, what he'd done when he'd gotten physically involved with Miranda. He felt a bit better after their conversation. At least they were on the same page, equally pulled between loyalty and love, attraction and desire, and, more than anything, the past and the future. If he had to continue to grapple with his history with Johnathon, at least he had a partner in all of this, one who understood for the most part where he was coming from.

After breakfast, he and Miranda got distracted from dishes yet again. He managed to say something that made her laugh, and the minute the happy sound hit his ears, he was overcome with his desire for her. He eased out of his chair and kneeled at her side, reaching for her face and pulling her lips to his. Their kiss was so soft and sexy he couldn't wait another minute. He tugged at the tie on her robe and peeled it back to reveal a silky black nightgown. With both thumbs, he pulled down the straps, freeing her full breasts. He cupped them in his hands, licked her nipples, flicking at the tight buds with his tongue and tasting the sweetness of her skin.

He slipped one hand between her legs, finding her wet for him. He moved his fingers in steady circles against her apex and she gasped for air between fiery hot kisses.

"I'm going to come," she blurted, breathless and frantic.

"I want you to," he said.

She grasped his wrist and looked him right in the eye. "So do I. But I want you inside me when I do."

She scrambled to her knees and he pulled off his pajama pants in a flash. With the silky nightgown around her waist, she straddled his hips, reached down for his erection and sank down onto his length. Her heat all around him, pulling him in, felt so good it boggled the mind. Meanwhile, the vision of her above him, the gentle bounce of her gorgeous breasts with every thrust, was nothing short of pure beauty on full display.

"I'm so close. Are you?" she asked. Her voice had a sexy rasp and he loved the fact that she'd been reduced to single-syllable words.

If only she knew that he nearly exploded as soon as he was inside her. "Yes. Just tell me and we'll come together."

She smiled and nodded, placing her hands flat on his chest and rolling her hips into his with determination, eyes closed and her raven hair splayed across the creamy skin of her bare shoulders. He nearly went blind as the pleasure circled and threatened to strike, but he focused on her face and the soft moans that came from her parted lips.

In one swift movement, she dropped her head forward. "Now."

He was so thankful for the go-ahead, and within fractions of a second, he was giving in to his release just as she called out, arched her back and whipped her long hair to the side. The waves kept crashing over him as he felt her body tighten and relax around him, over and over again.

She collapsed against his chest and kissed him softly. "That was one heck of a breakfast."

He laughed and pushed her hair back from her forehead, peering up at her stunning face. He wasn't sure he'd ever felt more lucky or more torn. She was more than everything he'd ever dared to wish for— she was a dream come true. But that meant he was going where he'd sworn he never would. He was falling for his brother's widow.

Eventually, they managed to peel themselves off the floor, and Miranda told him she'd take care of the kitchen if he wanted to shower. Andrew wanted to extend the invitation for her to join him, but he also knew he probably needed to slow things down at least a little. They had all weekend, after all. By the time he was dressed and headed back downstairs, she was on her way up.

"I'm going to throw on some clothes real quick, but if you want, you can bring out the boxes of decorations. Do you know where the storage area is? It's the door at the back of the utility room."

"Yeah. I got tools out of there when I put the crib together."

"Perfect. There are several stacks of red and green plastic tubs. They should all be together. I'll be back down in a minute to help." She popped up onto her toes and kissed him softly. "I'm excited, just so you know."

He laughed quietly to himself and proceeded with following orders, heading down the rest of the stairs and around to the utility room near the back of the house. The door to the storage space creaked when he opened it and he reached inside for the light switch on the wall. Several bare bulbs lit up the space, which thankfully had a full-height ceiling. The bins were immediately obvious, but there were a lot of them. A quick count told him more than twenty-five. He wasn't about to complain. This would be an adventure and it gave him this time with Miranda.

He quickly went to work, running two or three

bins at a time into the living room. There was more than enough space next to the soaring fireplace to stack everything. By the time Miranda arrived back downstairs, he was nearly done.

"Wow," she said. "You work fast."

He didn't have quite so many words right now—she was breathtaking in a creamy white sweater, which showed off her collarbone, and jeans, with her hair pulled back in a high ponytail. Her cheeks were flushed with pink, a beautiful afterglow, and he took a certain amount of pride in knowing that he'd put that color there.

"I aim to please," he said. "If you want to start digging through everything, I'll get the last load."

"Sounds like a plan."

When he returned to the storage space, something caught his eye—several old cardboard boxes labeled Baseball Cards. Both Johnathon and Andrew had collected them for a while when they were young. Although their generation was well beyond the golden age of collecting, it made it a very cheap hobby, which was a good thing since there was very little money around the Sterling household. They had no problem scoring shoeboxes full of cards at yard sales, often hundreds for only a few bucks.

Andrew peeled back the flaps of one of the boxes, spotting the cards in neat stacks. There was no telling how long they'd been sitting there, or whether Johnathon had even looked at them in recent years.

But it was a potent reminder of the life they had once shared and one of the few endeavors they enjoyed together. Once again, the guilt wound its way into his consciousness, but he would not let it ruin today. He closed the box, gathered the final crates for Miranda and made his way back into the living room.

"Are you okay?" Miranda asked as he set down the bins. She'd already pulled out garland, lights and big boxes of ornaments. "You look like you've seen a ghost."

Apparently, he hadn't quite shaken off that moment in the storage space. "I spotted a few boxes of baseball cards. It made me think of Johnathon."

"In a good way or a bad way?" The tone of her voice was so tentative it nearly broke his heart.

"I don't want to talk about it if it's going to upset you. This is supposed to be your day."

"Are you kidding me? I've been dying to know more about what you were like as kids. I could never get Johnathon to tell me." She put down a bundle of lights and stepped closer to him, looking up at him with her big brown eyes.

He surveyed the room, needing a break from that earnest expression on her face. It was a lot of pressure to have someone care that much about the countless memories he was holding on to so tightly. "Christmas was nothing in our house. Did Johnathon tell you that?" he asked, finally able to look at her again.

She shook her head. "No. He never said anything about it. Then again, we really only had two Christmases together between the year we were engaged and the year we were married."

"Our dad worked construction and he was injured when we were young. He got some disability and benefits through his union, but it was never enough to make up for the loss of income. That meant our mom had two jobs just to put food on the table. Between working and having to deal with two boys who were constantly fighting and roughhousing, there was no way she had enough energy to think about Christmas."

Miranda took his hand and led him to the couch. "Tell me more."

He felt the hesitation inside him, but there was something deeper, urging him to keep going. Miranda deserved to know these things. She deserved to understand some of what had brought him to this moment, and Christmas was the perfect illustration. "Our dad was no help. He was horribly bitter after his accident and it only got worse over the years. He spent most of his days watching the news and yelling at the TV. I honestly don't think he expressed any affection for our mom in the final years before he died."

"When was that?"

"Johnathon and I were both in high school."

"It's so sad."

"It is, but it's just the way things were. Everyone has parts of their past they don't like to think about." He shrugged. "But you can probably imagine what the dynamic in our house was like. Johnathon and I spent every minute walking on eggshells. Our dad had an explosive temper and our mom was just worn-out. That's how we ended up in such fierce competition. Johnathon was the oldest, so it was easy for him to manipulate me. I wanted his approval so desperately."

"Manipulate you how?"

"If he did something wrong, he always blamed it on me. Even if it was something that was so obviously his fault, like failing a test at school. He'd make up some story about how I'd distracted him while he was trying to study. He could never stand to be at fault or have anyone look at him in a negative light."

Miranda pressed her lips together tightly and nodded. "I saw that in him all the time. He always wanted to be the life of the party, and never the heavy."

"Exactly. And I took it because he was nicer to me when I did. He'd even say thank you for taking the heat. Only if we were outside or in our room, of course. Never in front of our parents."

"And that continued as you grew up?"

"Oh, no. It got worse. The older we got, the higher the stakes were. He got busted with pot, he drove our mom's car into a light pole. You name it."

"Wow. He really messed up a lot."

"Well, I was no angel. I got into trouble, too. But from where our parents were sitting, especially our mom after our dad died, I was the bad one and Johnathon was good. He used that to his advantage. It was sort of hard to blame him. I let him do it."

"Why?"

Andrew had asked himself this question countless times. He always came around to the same answer. "Because I loved him." He heard the crack in his voice as clear as day. It was an unwelcome sound. He didn't want to break. He never did.

"I'm so sorry."

He shook his head—if nothing else, it helped to ward off the sadness. "Does that help you see how we ended up the way we did? How fighting against each other just became our only dynamic? And because he seemed to care more about me the more I fought, I never managed to find another way to be with him."

"That's why you went after the Seaport. It was another fight to pick."

"Yes. Although I think it was Johnathon who started that. He knew exactly what he was doing when he went after that project. He knew it would hurt me."

"Because it was your hometown?"

Andrew swallowed hard, still not ready to tell her this. Then again, he wasn't sure how much time he and Miranda would have together and he was tired of living with regrets. "Because the wedding pavilion at the Seaport was where I was set to get married. And it didn't happen. Johnathon knew that. The whole idea of wanting to beautify that space and make it new again just felt very personal. It felt like an attack."

Miranda clasped her hand over her mouth. "I had no idea. What happened? With the wedding? With your fiancée?"

He took in a deep breath for strength. Rehashing this was not fun, but he did feel safe in sharing it with Miranda. "Oldest story in the book. She ran into an old boyfriend a few weeks before our wedding and she left me for him, but she didn't make that decision until the morning of the ceremony. I had to call the whole thing off. I never went back to the Seaport after that. And Johnathon knew how painful it was for me."

"That's why you felt so betrayed when you found out he decided to pursue the project. That's why you felt like you had to prevent it from happening."

"Yes." Now that he was admitting these things out loud, he wasn't sure if he should feel relieved or ashamed. There was a very big part of him that could look back and admit that he'd made some stupid choices. He had no direct knowledge that Johnathon had gone after the project to be cruel. It had only seemed like something he might do.

"I'm so sorry."

Andrew didn't want to let his sad story ruin their day. It was a good thing that he'd shared this with her. At least she could better understand his thought process and the events that had brought him to this moment. "Don't be sorry. It's in the past. I'd rather think about today." He got up and beelined for the mountain of storage boxes, opening one and pulling out a long strand of silvery garland. "I think it's time to get going on your decorating project."

Miranda hopped up from her seat. "We really don't have to if you don't want to."

"I wouldn't miss this for the world. All I ever wanted at Christmastime was some cheer and happiness."

Miranda lifted the lid from another bin and peered inside. "I don't know how cheery you'll be after we untangle all these Christmas lights."

He laughed and put his arm around her shoulder, leaning in to kiss her cheek. "I get you and the holidays today. I don't see how I end up being anything less than happy."

Eight

The Monday after Thanksgiving should've been like any other start to Miranda's workweek. She climbed into her car and headed to the office. The stereo was set to her favorite satellite radio station, playing a mix of pop and hits from her youth. The music was soft and in the background as she tried to focus on the day ahead. But today, she wasn't thinking about paint colors or special-order designer sofas. She wasn't ruminating over floor plans or deadlines. All she could think about was Andrew.

There was part of her that wondered if the events of the last few days had actually happened, even though she knew in her heart that they had. The echoes of his touch still warmed her skin, and the words he'd muttered into her ear still rang in her head. *If I kiss you, Miranda, there's no going back.* It was more than what he'd said, but how he'd said it that had really taken her breath away. The subtext was heavy. He wasn't about to make love to her then go back to simply being friends. But as for where that left them now, she wasn't sure.

She had never imagined this could happen. When she'd lost Johnathon, she'd thought that there would never be another man in her life. She'd seen herself becoming a mom and finding a way to parent on her own, but there would be no more romantic love. She simply couldn't have fathomed it in the aftermath of that tragedy. But with each passing day, things got a little better. She started to look ahead. Her grief changed from moment to moment, and it certainly wasn't always a straight line. But for the most part, she'd found the strength to move forward, in part because of those around her who loved her—Clay, Astrid, Tara and Grant.

But then Andrew had turned up and changed everything yet again. He'd awakened something in her, a part of her that she'd put aside as no longer viable. He'd made her feel like a woman again—desired and needed. He likely didn't understand the sheer scope of what he'd done, the switch that he had flipped, but it was no small thing. Right now, it meant the world to her.

She knew very well that she was playing a dangerous game with him, though. She needed him in her life. For her little girl, Andrew was more than an uncle. He was the only living extension of her father. Miranda would not deprive her child of knowing him. Which meant that she had to let Andrew know that she didn't expect anything of him. She couldn't saddle him with her feelings. What she had with Andrew was not a romance, even when her body believed it, her soul yearned for it, and there were tender and caring moments when she thought it was moving in that direction. It was...well, she struggled to put a label of any kind on it. And perhaps that was for the best. Labels came with expectations and that only led to disappointment.

She arrived at work and strode through the parking lot, noticing that Astrid's little silver convertible was already there. Miranda was really glad that she'd decided to hire her future sister-in-law. She was not only a hard worker, and eager to learn the business of interior design, but was also a positive presence in the office. Everyone on Miranda's team loved her and that gave Miranda a real sense of peace. Astrid could shoulder a lot of the workload in the weeks after the baby arrived. As for what the rest of Miranda's life would look like at that time, she didn't know. Could she count on the help of those around her? Would Andrew make his presence known? The uncertainty made her especially thankful for Astrid. She knew she could count on her.

"Good morning." Miranda popped her head into Astrid's office.

She looked up from her desk, a warm smile crossing her face. "Hello. How are you after the big Thanksgiving awkwardness?"

Miranda had been so horrified in the moment on Thursday evening, but it almost seemed like an afterthought now. If that situation hadn't happened, emotions wouldn't have been running so high that night. She and Andrew wouldn't have ended up kissing in the kitchen or even making love. Miranda gestured to one of the chairs opposite Astrid's desk. "May I?"

"Yes. Of course."

Miranda took a seat and crossed her legs. "That was something, wasn't it?"

"I wasn't there for the truly ugly part, but it's pretty obvious that Tara and Grant don't trust him. At all."

"So much of it seems like it should be water under the bridge, but obviously that's not the case."

"Andrew was well out of Johnathon's life when we were married," Astrid said.

"Same for me," Miranda said. "He talked about his brother, but it was all stuff that had happened in the past."

"It's really hard for me to say whether Andrew should be trusted, but he seems like a good person. Clay likes him a lot."

That counted for a great deal, as far as Miranda

was concerned. Her brother was an excellent judge of character. "It doesn't really matter though, does it? Andrew will be here for a short while and then he'll return to Seattle and that will be it." Miranda drew in a deep breath through her nose. "The problem is that I want more than that. I want him to be part of the baby's life. He'll be one of her few living relatives."

"Do you think you can count on him for that? Johnathon always said Andrew was erratic. He might seem solid right now, but you don't know for sure, right?" Astrid picked up a pen and tapped it on her desk. "I don't want to be pessimistic, but I also don't want to see you get hurt."

Miranda appreciated Astrid's intentions, but she hated the misgivings these questions stirred up inside her. Andrew had been nothing less than rock-solid over the last few weeks. He'd been caring and attentive. "I'm pretty sure that Johnathon was letting other things color his opinions. Like the history between the brothers. Andrew told me some stories over the weekend."

"Like what?"

"He talked about how Johnathon was the golden boy of the family. He was the one who could do no wrong. Andrew really looked up to him, but from everything he said, Johnathon used that against him. He blamed things on Andrew, but he'd later say that it was just part of their rivalry and that if Andrew didn't want to be in trouble, he should learn how to turn the tables on Johnathon."

"Was he ever able to do that?"

"Not to the degree he wanted to. Johnathon was always a step ahead."

"Until the Seaport Promenade project came along."

"Exactly. That was when Andrew finally saw his chance to get even." Miranda decided against sharing the details of Andrew's broken engagement. It was deeply personal and he'd kept it from Miranda for a while, even when he'd had chances to tell her and bring his motives into focus. "But then we lost Johnathon and Andrew had to try to stop his plan."

Astrid nodded slowly, as if she was still digesting all of this information. "Maybe Tara and Grant need to hear more of this. I don't think anyone can discount the fact that Clay likes him. That has to matter a lot, especially to you."

That was a silver lining, for sure. Her brother was deeply skeptical of most people. If it was Clay's gut instinct to trust Andrew, Miranda felt that she could, too. "And what do you think?"

"He's incredibly handsome and smart and kind. What's not to like?"

The corners of Miranda's lips twitched, threatening a smile, and heat flooded her cheeks. She couldn't have stopped if she'd wanted to. There wasn't a single thing not to admire about Andrew. Or at least not a thing that she'd seen.

Astrid narrowed her gaze on Miranda. She was incredibly perceptive, which made Miranda nervous. "Why do you have that look on your face?"

"What look? I don't know what you're talking about." The tone of her voice betrayed her. It was high and squeaky, like a little girl who was terrible at keeping secrets.

Astrid sat back in her chair and crossed her legs, pivoting left and right. "You don't have to tell me if you don't want to."

Miranda wanted to tell someone what had happened, but she also feared sharing it, especially with Astrid. What if she thought less of her? What if she thought Miranda hadn't let enough time transpire since Johnathon's death? "I'm afraid to tell you. If I'm being perfectly honest."

"You can always confide in me. I won't tell a soul. Not even Clay."

"I slept with him." The words practically shot out of Miranda's mouth.

Astrid's eyes grew impossibly wide with surprise. "With Andrew?"

"Who else would I possibly be talking about?"

Astrid stared off, nodding as if she was adding this all up. "I did notice you two flirting."

"You did?" Miranda was horrified. She'd thought

that any connection between her and Andrew was undetectable. Hidden.

"It's not a bad thing. I liked seeing it. I know how hard it's been for you. Dealing with Johnathon's death."

"Sleeping with his brother was probably not the healthiest way to chase away my grief."

Astrid shrugged. "You two have a very unusual connection, and you're living in the same house. It's not a big surprise to me that you were drawn to each other."

But where did all of that lead? Miranda had no earthly idea. And with a baby on the way, it was impossible for her to not think about the future. To fixate on it. Would it be okay if she and Andrew ultimately decided that they'd had a little fun together? Would she be able to maintain a relationship with him moving forward? Or would it always be uncomfortable and awkward, with sex as the elephant in the room?

Monday morning, soon after Miranda left for work, Andrew caught a break.

"I've found Sandy," Pietro said when Andrew answered his cell phone.

The relief that washed over him was immense. He had to get to Victor, and Sandy, Victor's foot soldier and one-time mole at Sterling Enterprises, was the best path. "Where is she?"

"She moved into an apartment downtown. It's a brand-new building. Not a lot of residents yet, but they have major security."

"Do you think we have any chance of getting to her?"

"Yes. We have found a way to access the garage and my guys have a good sense of her schedule. I'm outside the building right now."

Andrew grabbed his car keys from the desk. "I'll meet you."

"I have it under control, Mr. Sterling. I don't know that it's safe."

Andrew admired Pietro's dedication to protecting him, but Andrew was done caring about himself. He had to get to Victor. He had to find a way to convince him to stop. Andrew cared deeply about undoing the harm he'd done by setting the plan to destroy Sterling's chance at the Seaport Promenade project. But much more than that now, Miranda and the baby were the most important thing. He would not let them be hurt, physically or financially. More than that, he would not fail with the promises he'd made.

"I'll be fine," Andrew said. "Just ping me your location, okay?"

"Of course, Mr. Sterling."

Miranda and the baby were front and center in his thoughts as Andrew climbed into his car and zipped out through Miranda's gate. His heart was racing as he realized what it would mean if he got to Sandy and she was able to convince Victor to stop. He would have fixed the problem he'd created. He would also have no more reason to stay in San Diego with Miranda. The last few weeks had been incredible, a taste of the life he'd wanted so badly but couldn't help but think wasn't ultimately meant for him. It might be best to resolve everything, move on and leave Miranda to her life. But if he did that, it would be the hardest thing he'd ever done. There was a nagging sense that it wasn't the answer, but it was certainly the simplest solution—get through the pain and move past it.

He found Pietro on a side street. "Any sign of her?" Andrew asked as he climbed out of his car and met him on the sidewalk.

"She should be pulling out of the garage soon. We have surveillance that says she just left her apartment."

"What are we waiting for?" Andrew asked, starting across the street.

"I was waiting on you." Pietro jogged behind him to catch up.

At the garage entrance was a keypad. Pietro punched in a code and the metal door rolled up. Andrew made a mental note to give the man a raise. He never failed to amaze him. Inside, it was evident the building was both brand-new and for only the most well-heeled. Everything was pristine. It was more like a waiting room for cars, with no evidence of smells like motor oil or gasoline.

"Put on your sunglasses," Pietro suggested. "It'll be harder to ID you on tape."

Smart. Pietro was on it, as usual. Andrew did as he was told and the men strode through the concrete structure until they reached the elevator. Sure enough, a mere moment after they arrived, the lights above the door indicated that someone was heading down.

"I don't want to scare her," Andrew said. He'd been the one to hire Sandy. He did know her pretty well and he couldn't help but think that she had become a pawn in a game that was far outside her control.

"Of course not. It's merely my job to put you in a position to speak to her."

"Perfect. Thank you."

Seconds later, the door dinged and rolled open. Sandy took one look at Andrew and her already pale skin lost all color. Her eyes went wide and she jabbed the button. Pietro was one step ahead and stuck out his foot, preventing the door from closing and causing it to open again.

"I have nothing to say to you," she blurted at Andrew as he stepped closer. Her dark hair was styled in a new way, cut in a sleek and sophisticated bob.

"Fine. You don't need to talk to me. I just need you to relay a message to your new boss."

"That's it?" She seemed unconvinced.

"That's it."

Sandy rolled her eyes and breezed past him and Pietro, into the garage. The door slid shut behind her. "Then what's the message?" She turned and faced him defiantly. She had a very large designer handbag hanging from her elbow. Victor was obviously compensating her well.

"Tell Victor that I will pay him ten million to go away. That's twice what he lost in his deal with Johnathon."

Sandy did not appear impressed by that number. "Where does that leave me?"

"Victor's the person who should answer that question. I'm no longer your employer."

"And if you really want me to deliver this message, you should probably pay the messenger her own fee."

"Fine. An extra million straight to you."

"I could spend that in three months. This building is ridiculously expensive. Try harder."

"Two?"

She pressed her lips together tightly, but everything in her eyes said she wasn't stressed. She was calculating. "Four."

This was becoming absurd. "If I give you four and Victor finds out about it, he'll only ask me for more."

"You're a very rich man."

"Twenty to Victor. Five to you. Final offer."

Sandy swallowed hard. Finally some sign that he was getting somewhere. "I'll take it to him. No promises."

"Please let him know that I'd like to hear from him today."

"I will." She clicked a key fob and the lights on a shiny black Audi flashed.

"So he's in town?" he asked.

"Nice try. I'm not telling you where he is." She put her sunglasses on, then reached for the car's door handle. "And please don't do this little act again. I don't appreciate you showing up where I live."

"Fair enough."

Andrew and Pietro watched as Sandy got into her car. They waited for her to leave before following through the open garage door and back outside. Moments later, they were at their vehicles across the street.

"Only thing we can do now is wait," Andrew said.

"You'll let me know if you hear anything?" Pietro asked.

"Absolutely." Andrew climbed into his car and pulled away from the curb, heading back to Miranda's. He was nearly there when his phone rang. The caller ID popped up on the screen on his dash. *Unknown caller.* He took the call, anyway. "Hello?"

"You must be getting desperate," the voice said.

Victor. "What makes you say that?" Andrew did his best to maintain his composure.

"You're trying to bribe me. Which I can only guess means that you are getting close to your brother's widow. Miranda, right?"

Andrew's stomach turned. Waves of nausea rolled over him. He didn't ever want to hear Victor utter Miranda's name again. "That's not why I made the offer. I just want this done."

"You must realize that money does no good. I couldn't spend everything I already have if I tried."

Andrew needed to focus on this conversation, which meant he needed to get off the road. He flipped his blinker and took the next exit, pulling onto a side street. He put the car in Park and killed the engine. "It's not about the money. It's about making up for my brother's mistake. It's the principle."

"Mistakes. Plural. It was more than the five million I lost in that deal that you know about. That was the final insult. There was another forty or fifty before that. And the lies. Your brother left a wake of destruction wherever he went."

Andrew was looking at paying a small fortune if he wanted to appease Victor, but he would do anything to finally have it resolved. To have a chance to look at his future and see some possibilities for happiness. "What do you want? Name your price."

Victor laughed. "What I want, you can't give me. Unless you come back to my side."

Andrew pinched the bridge of his nose as a headache sprang up right behind his eyes. "I don't know what you're talking about."

"I want Sterling Enterprises destroyed. Over. Erased."

Andrew blew out an exasperated breath. "Johnathon's dead. What's the point?"

"The point is that Sterling is going to land the Seaport project and Johnathon's picture is going to be all over the place. His firm will win accolades and awards. They're hoping to get the new playground at Seaport named after him. It will be like he never did a single bad thing and that's not right."

"But you're only punishing the people he left behind."

"You mean like his wives? And his business partner, Grant Singleton?"

"Well, yes. That's exactly who I mean." He wasn't about to mention the baby, but Andrew's niece would also be a victim. He was sure Victor knew that Miranda was pregnant, but Andrew didn't want to call attention to it.

"This way, they will all know that Johnathon wasn't the perfect man they all think he was."

Andrew's frustration was growing by the minute. "Why do you care so much? This just seems like it's about more than money and ego."

"Johnathon seduced my daughter when she was only twenty years old. He broke her heart. He made promises to her and he didn't keep a single one. I can't forgive him for that. Never."

Andrew stared straight ahead at the city scene before him—a busy Mexican restaurant and people milling around on the sidewalk—but it was like he wasn't truly seeing any of it. He was too busy grappling with this revelation. "When did this happen?"

"He was married to the second wife."

"Astrid."

"That's her name."

Andrew shook his head in disbelief. There was a very big part of him that was so tired of cleaning up his brother's messes. But he knew that this one wouldn't simply go away. "I'm sorry. I don't know what to say about your daughter. I didn't know that happened. Why in the world did you keep working with him after that happened?"

"I kept hoping that at some point, I would have a chance to get back at Johnathon with one of our deals. Screw him over. Unfortunately, he always seemed to be a step ahead of me. I don't like it when that happens. I don't like being made to look like a fool."

Andrew felt like he was out of options. "What do you want me to do, Victor? This needs to end. I'll give you whatever you want. You can have every last penny I have in the bank."

"I have a few tricks up my sleeve. If they pan out, I'll go away. I just want to see a few people squirm.

If I can't bury Sterling Enterprises, I can at least hurt them badly."

The line went dead. The display on Andrew's dashboard said "call ended."

Andrew could've easily sat there and felt sorry for himself, but one word wouldn't stop echoing in his head—*them*. That sounded personal. Andrew had to warn someone at Sterling about what might be coming down the pike. The logical person was Grant. Maybe Tara. But after the scene at Thanksgiving, Andrew wanted to speak to someone whom he knew would actually listen. He needed some help from Clay.

Nine

Andrew raced to Sterling Enterprises feeling uncertain but determined. He'd had a hopeful conversation with Clay, one that made him feel as though he had a true ally at the company. That would be important as he found a way past this.

Andrew's central concerns always revolved around Miranda and the baby—keeping them safe and happy. He couldn't make peace with his brother, but he could take care of the people Johnathon had left behind. Part and parcel of his duty would be finding a peaceful way to stay in Miranda's life. At the very best, he couldn't let his relationship with the people in Miranda's life get any worse. He had to keep Clay and Astrid on his side, and he had to find a way to make Tara and Grant trust him. They didn't have to like him. That might never happen. But Andrew did not want his existence in her world to bring pain or stress to Miranda. She'd been through enough.

"Andrew Sterling for Clay Morgan," he said to the receptionist when he arrived at the Sterling offices, near the top of a downtown skyscraper.

"Andrew," Clay called, emerging from a corridor to the right. He offered a handshake, followed by an inquisitive look. "You doing okay? You look rattled."

Was it that obvious? "I've been better. I'd like to catch you up on everything."

"Yeah. Of course. We'll talk in my office." Clay led Andrew through the serpentine maze that was Sterling Enterprises, the empire built by his brother. The specter of Johnathon didn't feel as overwhelming here, and for that, Andrew was grateful. "Here we are," Clay said.

"Thanks." Andrew was glad they'd reached the safe haven of Clay's office without encountering Tara or Grant. He didn't want a scene. He'd had his fill on Thanksgiving.

Clay closed the door and rounded behind his desk. "Please. Have a seat."

Andrew sat at one end of a black leather sofa and decided to get right to it. "I spoke to Victor. I attempted to pay him off to keep him from his attempts at sabotaging Sterling, but he refused to listen. My guess is that he'll make another run at messing with your chances on the Seaport project, but there's a chance he'll try something else."

"Like what?"

If only Andrew knew the answer to that question. It would make life so much easier. "No idea. I only know that he's really out for vengeance. He lost quite a bit more money to Johnathon than I ever knew. North of fifty million."

"Ouch."

"And it gets worse. There's a personal aspect to his mission." Andrew hesitated to offer more. This news would impact Clay because of his relationship with Astrid.

"What kind of personal?"

Andrew cleared his throat and decided the most direct approach was the best. "Johnathon seduced Victor's daughter when she was twenty. He broke her heart. This was several years ago, but Victor's still very angry about it. His daughter seems to mean the world to him."

Unmistakable concern was painted all over Clay's face. "I understand. I feel the same way about my daughter."

"Of course." Andrew's thoughts were drawn to Miranda's baby. She hadn't even been born yet and he already felt extremely protective of her. He could imagine the fierce anger that would crop up if he discovered that anyone had hurt her in the same way Johnathon had hurt Victor's daughter.

"Okay. I get it. He's out for blood. Or as close as he can get to it."

"Exactly. But you should know there's one more important detail to this story. Johnathon did this while he was married to Astrid."

Clay sucked in a sharp breath. It was like he'd taken a punch to the gut, but of course he felt that way. He loved Astrid. Anything that hurt her, hurt him, too. "Wow." He set his elbow on his chair's armrest and ran his hand through his hair, shaking his head in disbelief. "She will be so hurt when she finds out. Or we need to think about whether she needs to know at all."

"I won't say a thing. That's up to you to decide."

"What do we do now?"

Andrew sincerely wished he had a plan that went beyond waiting to see what Victor might do next. "We have to be hypervigilant. And since his primary target is Sterling, that means watching everything here very closely."

"I can't do that on my own. I simply don't have involvement with every project we're working on."

Andrew knew what came next. "Right. Which is why we need to put Grant and Tara in the loop. The problem is I doubt they'll listen to me."

Clay rapped a knuckle on his desktop. "All we can do is try." He picked up his office phone and pressed a button. "Grant. Hey. It's Clay," he said. "Can I steal a few minutes with you and Tara? It's important."

Andrew's stomach wobbled with uncertainty, but he had to get past this. Ultimately, he was on the same side as Tara and Grant. He just needed to prove it to them.

Clay nodded. "Great. We'll be there in a sec. I have Andrew with me." He dropped the handset back into the cradle like it was a hot coal. "I decided not to give him a chance to yell at me now."

"Smart." *Might as well let him save his ire for me.*

Clay and Andrew headed over to Grant's office. That meant crossing a large open area of people working at desks, a bullpen of sorts. Andrew attracted curious glances with every step. His resemblance to Johnathon had to be the reason, but that realization did nothing to calm his nerves. It was yet another reminder that he'd spent his life in his brother's shadow, and getting out from behind it might never be possible.

Clay hesitated at the doorway to Grant's office, but they were quickly welcomed in. Tara was already there, perched on the arm of an upholstered chair opposite Grant's desk. Her posture said she was ready for battle, her arms crossed defiantly. Grant was settled in his high-backed leather chair, like a king overseeing his domain. Silence fell as Clay closed the door behind him and he and Andrew ventured farther inside. Neither Grant nor Tara invited them to sit, and that was probably for the best. Andrew did not want to stay.

"Okay, then." Clay clapped his hands together once. "Andrew has some developments regarding Victor."

Tara was already shaking her head. "I hope this is going to be quick."

Andrew's patience was already gone, but he wasn't about to lose his temper. He'd deliver this news in as cool and dispassionate a manner as he could. "You don't have to listen to me. But I hope you will." He launched into everything he'd just told Clay, but he kept the detail about Astrid to himself. He wanted that information kept to the smallest circle possible. When he was finished, Grant and Tara remained unimpressed.

"What exactly do you want us to do?" Grant asked.

"That's up to you, but I suggest you keep tight control of everything. No new hires. Brief your security team. Your IT department, as well. Watch who's coming in and out of the office, and who's getting access to the company's computer servers. More than anything, keep an eagle eye on the Seaport project. That's still his most likely target."

"Once again, we have to wonder if this is all a cover for you pursuing a scheme that you started," Tara said.

"What do I have to gain from lying to you? I want this to be done as much as anyone."

"So you can leave town?" Grant asked.

Andrew's stomach sank at the thought of that. He might not be welcome in this room, or in other parts of Miranda's life, but when it was just the two of them, alone, he felt like he had a glimpse of the life he'd always wanted. He didn't want to turn his back on that, but how could he ever prove himself in these circles? For years, Johnathon had poisoned Grant and Tara to the very idea of Andrew. That was a fact. It would take time for Andrew to turn this ship around. He couldn't expect that to happen overnight, and it certainly wouldn't happen until he could prove Victor's existence. That might mean a painful outcome and waiting until Victor pounced.

Andrew looked at Clay. "I've said all I needed to say. I'll show myself out." He turned to Tara and Grant. "Thanks for your time." He had to find a way to be above it all.

Andrew marched through the bullpen, trying to ignore the repeated stares. He'd nearly crossed the space when Clay caught up with him.

"Wait. Hold up," Clay said. "Are you okay?"

Andrew kept walking until they were in a quiet section of the hall. "Yeah. Fine. It's just more of the same."

Clay clapped Andrew's arm. "I'm sorry. Don't worry. It'll all get worked out."

If only Andrew could be so sure. "Thank you. I appreciate that you have any confidence in me at all."

"Of course. Thank you for being there for my sister."

That made Andrew feel one hundred times better. Miranda was the reason to fight. "No need to thank me. I'm happy to do it."

Outside on the street, Andrew pulled his phone out of his pocket and immediately called Miranda. It wasn't that he wanted to dump all of this on her. He just needed to hear her voice.

"Hey there," she answered. "This is a nice surprise. Everything okay at the house?"

Andrew strode down the city sidewalk to his car, which was parked near the corner. It was chilly being in the shadow of the tall buildings around him, but thoughts of Miranda kept him warm. "Everything at the house is fine. I actually just came from the Sterling offices."

"You did? Why?"

Andrew clicked the fob and climbed into his car. "I didn't have a choice." He gave Miranda the abbreviated version of his morning, without the detail about Astrid. "So that's where we stand. It looks like I'm going to be in San Diego indefinitely. I hope that's okay. I'm happy to move back into the hotel."

"Andrew. Don't be silly. I want you staying with me. I need you there."

Heat rose in his body, especially his face. "Good. Because that's where I want to be."

"Maybe you can stay through Christmas. That would be nice."

The idea of that made Andrew incredibly happy, but he didn't want to get too far ahead of himself. *One day at a time.* "If that's the way the calendar works out, I will try to stay."

"So you weren't able to make any progress with Tara and Grant? Mend any fences?"

"No. I'd say things are pretty much the same."

"Oh." She sounded nothing short of disappointed, making Andrew feel as though he'd failed.

"Are you surprised?"

"Not necessarily. I guess I was just being hopeful."

Andrew laughed. He couldn't help it. At this point, the idea was absurd, but Miranda often wore rose-colored glasses. "What about that situation would give you hope?"

"Maybe it was more wishful thinking."

"Why's that?"

"Because I'm hoping you'll be my date for Grant and Tara's wedding."

"Really?" Andrew would have gone anywhere with Miranda, but attending Tara and Grant's nuptials was the absolute last thing he wanted to do.

"Yes, really. Astrid and I are the bridesmaids and I don't want to go by myself."

"You don't want a pariah for a date. It'll be like Thanksgiving all over again."

"Oh, shush. You're perfect. And I love the thought of being on your arm."

Something inside him melted. How could he say no? He couldn't, even when the list of his reservations about attending Grant and Tara's wedding was a mile long. "Okay, then. I guess I'd better rent a tux."

Miranda nearly didn't answer the phone when Tara called on Friday. Between Andrew's unpleasant chat with her and Grant at Sterling earlier that week, and the lecture she'd given Andrew on Thanksgiving, Tara was not her favorite person. But Miranda had been home from work for an hour now and was looking forward to a relaxing weekend with Andrew. She hoped that Tara was ready to let cooler heads prevail.

Miranda answered the call on speaker. "Hello?"

"Everything is ruined," Tara blurted. "Absolutely everything." It almost sounded as if Tara was crying, which really put Miranda on notice. Tara did *not* cry. "The wedding has been cancelled."

"Did something happen with Grant?"

"No. We're fine. It's not that. It's our plans. Everything I've spent months working on is ruined."

That made no sense, but Miranda was sure this was normal bridal jitters. It was two weeks until the wedding. Perfectly understandable that Tara would be worked up about it. "Take a deep breath. Tell me what happened."

"Someone phoned the venue and said we'd called off the engagement. Same thing for the florist and the caterers. Even the tuxes were canceled."

"What? How does that happen?"

"I don't know. It happened some time on Monday, but nobody bothered to tell me. We'd already lost our deposits, so I guess they didn't care? I tried to reach the caterer to give them the final numbers for entrées, and that's when I found out. Then I started making other calls and it turns out that the whole thing is ruined. I don't know what I'm supposed to do."

"There has to be a way to fix this. I'll help."

Andrew walked into the room and looked at Miranda inquisitively. She pushed the mute button on her phone to prevent Tara from hearing what she was about to say. "It's Tara. Someone canceled her wedding. How weird is that?"

Andrew stuffed his hands into his pants, shaking his head. "I don't have a good feeling about this."

"Hold on. I'd better get back on the line or Tara will freak." Miranda turned off the mute button. "Once again, take a deep breath. We can fix this." As to why any of this was Miranda's problem, she wasn't sure, but it was her inclination to help.

"What if Andrew did this?" Tara asked.

Miranda deeply regretted leaving Tara on speaker.

Andrew was still standing right there. "I know you're upset, but that's ridiculous. Why would he do that when he's been trying everything he can to earn your trust?"

Andrew threw up his hands and bounded out of the room. Now Miranda had two sets of ruffled feathers to smooth, but at least she had an excuse to take Tara off speaker.

"Because it's affecting the business. There's a big story on one of the business-news websites saying that Grant and I have called off our engagement and the company is in trouble because the two most senior people are at odds. Our shareholders have been calling Grant nonstop."

"Does that really sound like something Andrew would do? Because I don't think it does."

"You're blind to all of this, Miranda. You two are sleeping together, aren't you?"

It had only been a matter of time before this news got out, but it still didn't make it a more comfortable topic of conversation. "How do you know that? Did Astrid tell you?"

"So you *are* having sex." She said it in such a deeply accusatorial tone. "I was just guessing. There's entirely too much solidarity between you two. I sensed that at Thanksgiving."

"Solidarity? We're helping each other through a difficult time. If that's a crime, then I guess I'm guilty as charged, but I'm not going to apologize for it. I'm a grown woman and this is my life."

"Do you have any idea how much this would upset Johnathon?"

Miranda's heart skipped a beat, and not in a good way. It was like being plunged into ice-cold water. That was an *extremely* low blow. How dare Tara ask that question? "Of course I know, Tara. I was still his wife when he died. You were not."

Several moments of silence played out on the other end of the line. It seemed like an eternity, and Miranda already felt bad for what she'd said, but she was tired of being on the receiving end of so much disrespect. Either directly or indirectly, so many people had suggested to Miranda that they'd known Johnathon better than she had. Yes, their marriage had been a short one, and Miranda hadn't been around long enough to know every detail of Johnathon's life before her, but that didn't mean they hadn't been close. She might not have been privy to every shred of his history, but she'd known what he had in his heart for her.

"Oh, God. I'm so sorry, Miranda. I don't know what got into me."

"I need you to understand something. Every day, I deal with the ghost of Johnathon and the question of what he would have wanted or not wanted. I want to honor him. I do. But I'm also the person who's left on earth after him. I want a life, Tara. It might have felt like I died the same day Johnathon did, but that's not permanent. I don't have the luxury of staying in that frame of mind. This baby is going to be here before we know it. She needs me to look forward. To the future. And try to see the possibilities."

"You're so right. And I'm truly sorry. Can you forgive me?"

"Can you start putting a little faith in Andrew? Because I know with every fiber of my being that he would not cancel someone's wedding and he certainly wouldn't plant some fake, gossipy story. That's just not him."

"You really do trust him, don't you?"

Just then, Andrew walked back into the room. He was wearing that look of deep concern, the one that was so often painted on his face. She truly hoped that one day soon, the weight of all of this could be off his shoulders. He didn't deserve to carry the burden.

"I do trust Andrew," Miranda said, catching his eye. "One hundred percent."

For a moment, the expression on Andrew's face lightened, his eyes flashing with their deep brilliance. "Thank you," he whispered.

"Tara, I need to go. What can I do to help with this wedding fiasco? I have to think the venue is your first concern. Can't you or Grant put some pressure on them? Surely you know someone over there."

"It's not a matter of pressure. This close to Christmas, the space is in high demand. It's gone. But maybe that part of it is for the best. I never wanted a big wedding, and we kept the guest list small. I think I've convinced Grant that we should just get married at the house."

"That's a wonderful idea. You couldn't ask for a more beautiful setting. What about the flowers? Other decorating and rentals? You'll need chairs. Have you thought about a tent? I'm happy to handle any of that. I have contacts through my design business."

"Really? After what I said about Johnathon?"

Miranda wasn't sure if she was being naive, but something was telling her to keep pushing her agenda of mending these ties for Andrew. When this baby arrived, she wanted her world to be harmonious, or as close to that as she could get. "Yes. I really want to help."

"If you could tackle the flowers and rentals, that would take a big weight off my shoulders. I can deal with the caterers and everything else."

"That works. Can you send me some details about what you wanted? I'll make a few phone calls to let people know we need them on that date. December nineteenth, right?"

"That much has not changed. You're wonderful, Miranda. Thank you."

"You're like a sister to me, Tara. Sometimes you're a pain in the butt, but that doesn't mean I don't love you and care about your happiness."

"I love you, too. I want you to be happy, too."

"Good. Because I need you to know that Andrew is my date for the wedding. And I need that to not be a problem, okay?"

Tara sucked in a deep breath. Miranda could hear it over the line. "Got it."

"I'm serious. I want you to tell Grant, too."

"I'm on it. Believe me, I don't want that day to be anything short of perfect."

"Me, too, Tara. Me, too." Miranda ended the call and tossed aside her phone. "Well, that was an ordeal."

"I only heard part of the conversation. Tara and Grant's wedding plans were canceled?"

"Yes. And there's a gossipy story on the internet saying they've split up and it's making things bad at Sterling."

Andrew wagged his head from side to side. "It has to be Victor. He said that if he couldn't destroy Sterling, he wanted to hurt them."

"You mean *it*."

Andrew again shook his head. "I specifically remember him saying *them*. That's personal. You don't get much more personal than ruining someone's wedding."

"And it's Grant and Tara. The two most senior people at the company."

"It's a twofer. A direct hit. One more reason I have to stop Victor."

"Any ideas?"

"When you were on the phone with Tara, I was in the other room trying to reach Sandy. I had to leave a message. No telling when or if she'll call me back."

"So we wait?"

"We don't have a choice right now. I told Tara and Grant to be watching everything, but I was talking about the company. It's understandable that they weren't focused on the wedding plans they thought were firmly in place."

Miranda got up from her seat on the sofa, drawn to Andrew, like always. "I told her you're my date. And I was very specific that everyone needs to be on their best behavior."

He gazed down into her eyes and once again, she felt as though she might never understand the complexity hidden behind them. "That shouldn't have to be said. You shouldn't have to defend me. I hate that it demands anything of you at all, other than to RSVP *yes*."

"I can't help it. It just comes naturally to me. And I know they'll come around. They will."

He gripped her forearm and tugged her closer, combing his fingers into her hair. "What makes you the way you are, Miranda Sterling? You have every reason in the world to be bitter and angry, but you never give in to it. I could learn a lot about generosity and forgiveness from you."

"You're sweet." Her heart felt like it was jumping around like a droplet of water on a hot skillet. She wanted him to take her upstairs and take off her clothes, so she could feel his hands all over her body. She needed him. She wanted him. And it would happen. But she had to make a few phone calls first. She'd promised. "If you want to learn some more about generosity, you can help me fix Tara and Grant's wedding."

Ten

Miranda was on wedding-repair duty, but Andrew was trying to help. He was on his laptop in her home office, sifting through the lengthy emails Tara had forwarded to Miranda, detailing everything from flowers to something called swags. He didn't want to be a guy about it, but he was in a bit over his head.

"That's the last call." Seated at her desk, Miranda jabbed at her cell phone once, then put it down. "Did you get anywhere with Tara's wish list?"

"I don't even know what half of this stuff is."

"Like what?" There was a flirtatious edge to her voice that took him by surprise. She got up from her desk and walked over to where he was sitting, on the small love seat in her office.

"Like a swag." He pointed to the email on his laptop.

She pushed down the screen until his computer was closed up. "Remember how we hung the strands of silver bells and garland above the doorway in the living room when we decorated for Christmas? That's a swag. For the wedding, it'll just be some fabric. It softens the rough edges." Her grin was equal parts come-hither and shy. Her cheeks flushed with a breathtaking shade of pink, a lighter color than her lips. It was hopelessly inviting. All he could think was that *she* softened *his* rough edges.

"No more volunteer work for Grant and Tara."

She stood before him in the same blue dress he'd seen her in when she'd left for work that morning, but somehow he hadn't taken the time to really notice the way it hugged every inch of her gorgeous body, or the way it brought out her deep brown eyes.

"You look absolutely gorgeous," he said, craving her touch. Their gazes naturally found each other and the electricity between them was hard to fathom, like an entire year of a power plant's output encapsulated in that moment. He was shocked that the current arcing between them wasn't visible.

"Thank you." Her head tilted to the side, only a fraction of an inch, but he loved seeing the way she was willing to show him the subtle hints that he'd said the right thing. "You don't look half-bad yourself." She stepped closer, peering down at him. She was conveying a most intriguing mix of business and play. If she wanted to get serious about playing with him, he was up for that.

She tugged on his hand and he stood. Her hands pressed hard against his chest, smoothing the fabric of his dress shirt. He watched her, smiling, their eyes again connecting. It looked as if there was a fire blazing behind hers—wild and intense. Which one of them would give in to the kiss first? He had no idea. He only knew that he would win either way.

"I want things to be good between us, Miranda. I don't want us to be lugging around so much baggage. It doesn't feel fair." He felt a burning need to bring up the state of their relationship, however much it was tenuous and defied definition. This was the price of wanting to make love to a woman who had once been married to his brother. He was treading on hallowed ground.

"I agree. I don't want anything else between us." Her lips parted ever so slightly and a gentle rush of air passed from them. It was the sound of pressure being released. "Including clothes." Her hands hadn't left his chest. She leaned into him, and her fingers played with the buttons of his shirt. "I vote that we don't worry about anything more than you and me and the evening we have stretching out before us."

He grinned again, this time much more eagerly.

"You're smiling," she said.

"Of course I am. It's impossible to not be happy

around you. Even when it's been a terrible day, you bring it out of me."

He snaked his hand around her waist and settled it in the curve of her lower back. Her lips traveled closer to his, but she stopped shy of a kiss, humming instead, the vibration sending waves of anticipation to his mouth. She flicked open one of the buttons of his shirt. Only one. This was quickly turning into a game of undressing, and as much as he loved a slow seduction, he wanted her naked. He reached up for the zipper of her dress, then pulled it down the center of her back as she finally started to rush through his shirt buttons. He longed to see the stretch of her skin revealed by the open zipper, so he turned her around, admiring her creamy skin as it contrasted with a black bra. He continued with the downward motion of the metal closure, his breath catching when he caught sight of her lacy panties. He eased the dress from her shoulders, savoring every sensory pleasure—her smell, the heat that radiated from her, her smooth skin as he dragged the back of his hand along the channel of her spine. Her presence didn't merely have him primed. He was already perilously close to the brink.

The garment slipped down the length of her body to the floor and she cast a seductive look back at him, her eyes deep, warm and craving. "A lot less between us now."

Oh, yes. He grasped her shoulders and pinned her

back to his chest, then wrapped his arms around her waist. He reached down and caressed the soft roundness of her belly as she craned her neck. He kissed her with some force—enough so that she would never question how much he wanted her. He cupped one of her breasts, the silky fabric of her bra teasing his palm as her skin tightened beneath his touch. Their tongues tangled and Miranda turned herself in his arms. He wrangled himself out of his shirt and pants with some help from her. It was a frantic and hurried blur. They were both eager to get to the main event. He pulled her close when he was naked and kissed her again. Miranda cast aside any sweetness for a demanding edge he wanted to satisfy.

With a pop, he unhooked her bra and quickly teased it from her body. He took her breasts in his hands and Miranda's eyes fluttered shut as his thumbs rubbed back and forth against her dark pink, firm nipples. The gasp that came from her when he flicked his tongue against her tight skin was music to his ears.

She bent to one side to step out of her panties. Her beautiful bare body heightened his awareness of how badly he wanted to claim her. There was no way they'd make it upstairs. At least not until later. He sat on the love seat, half-reclining, and reached out his hand.

"Come here. I need you."

She smiled and cocked an eyebrow, taking his hand. "No bedroom?"

"Not this first time. We have all night. For upstairs."

"Are you that impatient?"

"In a word, yes." The breath caught in his chest as he watched her carefully set her knee next to his hip and straddle him. The sky outside had fully fallen into darkness, but the glow from the lamp on her desk was just bright enough to show off the dips and hollows of her delicate collarbone. He traced his fingers along the contours.

She smiled, dropping her head to kiss him. Her silky hair brushed the sides of his face. He was almost sorry he didn't have the visual of the moment she took him in her hand, guided him inside and began to sink down around him. A deep groan escaped his throat as her body molded around him, warm and inviting. He couldn't think of another place on earth he'd rather be.

She settled her weight on his and they moved together in a dance he wanted to go on forever. He couldn't believe that this beautiful, sweet woman would ever want him. She rocked her hips into his, again and again, as they kissed and his hands cradled her velvety, perfect bottom. He was already in such ecstasy that it felt as if his body was floating, but he would've been lying if he'd said that his heart wasn't heavy. This happened every time they made love.

Every time she gave of herself like this. He'd done the unthinkable. He'd fallen for his dead brother's wife. There was no unringing that bell.

Miranda's breaths quickened and before he knew what was happening, she was gathering around him in steady pulses. It was enough to pull him out of his more serious thoughts and mercifully push him into the moment. She sat back, their eyes connecting for an instant, then she gave in to the sensation fully, closing her eyes and knocking her head back. He shut his own eyes and the relief shuddered out of him. Either he was dreaming, or each passing wave brought them closer.

Miranda felt worn-out, yet light as air. She collapsed against Andrew's chest, still struggling to catch her breath as a few echoes of the pleasure washed over her. There had been a moment in the midst of their lovemaking that he'd slipped away from her. He'd seemed disengaged. It probably only lasted for a second or two, and it was insignificant in terms of what they'd just done together, but it still made her concerned.

"Are you okay?" She sat back and cradled both sides of his head, peering straight into his eyes.

He laughed quietly, his eyes not quite open all the way. "Are you kidding me? I'm better than okay. I'm magnificent. You're amazing."

He brought his lips to her bare shoulder and it

reminded her body of the things he could do to her with just a single touch. Her nipples grew hard again. Her center ached for more of him, even when she was straddling his lap and there were no clothes between them.

"Okay. It's just that there was a moment when it felt like you weren't here. It's not a big deal. And maybe it's my pregnancy brain. I swear it doesn't work the way it used to. I just wanted to be sure that everything's okay."

"Sure."

"You can tell me anything, you know."

He grinned. "You love to push it, don't you?"

She shrugged. "I don't like leaving things unsaid."

He nodded and pulled her closer until she had no choice but to settle her head on his shoulder. Perhaps this was easier for him, when they didn't have to look each other in the eye. His fingers traveled gracefully up and down her back, lulling her into peacefulness. Still, she sensed that there was something between them, and she'd just told him that she didn't want that to be the case.

"This isn't easy, Miranda, but I feel stupid even saying that. It's not like you don't already know that. It's not like you don't experience that every day."

She sensed what he was about to say next, and it brought a tear to her eye.

"Like it or not, the reality of our situation is that Johnathon brought us together. He's the reason we're here alone. It's difficult for me to come to terms with that. I have to wonder if the guilt will always be there."

Miranda pushed back so she could see his face. She wanted him to understand that she was just as torn as he was. "I know. There are times when I can look beyond it and moments when I can't. But I don't want guilt to dictate what happens between us." She felt foolish for saying that, but the truth was that she was a widow who was expecting a baby. Her life was flat-out serious. That was all there was to it. She could act like things were of little consequence, but that wasn't where she was.

"I don't want it to, either. I'm just telling you that's the struggle I'm going through right now. But I don't want to burden you with that. You have enough to worry about, between the baby and work and now having to deal with Tara and Grant's wedding."

"How did I get sucked into that, anyway?"

"You're too nice. That's how."

"Um, not entirely true. I stood up to Tara today. She knows we're…" She waved her hands around. "Doing this."

"Having sex?"

"Yes. I asked her if Astrid told her, but it turns out that she guessed."

"Astrid knows, too? How did that happen?"

Miranda felt the heat rise in her cheeks. "I couldn't help it. We were talking about all of the Thanksgiving drama on Monday and it just sort of slipped out. Are you mad?"

"I'm assuming this means your brother also knows."

Miranda shrugged. "Probably." She hadn't given that too much thought, but it was logical. Astrid and Clay were very open with each other. "It's a good thing, if you think about it. He still likes you."

Andrew let loose one of his unguarded laughs. They didn't come often, but Miranda loved it when they did. "He said he likes me because I take care of you."

"He's right. I was not a happy camper before you moved in."

"I find that very hard to believe. I mean, I know you're still in mourning, but you're so upbeat."

Miranda thought about the many days where it was nearly impossible to roll out of bed, or the mornings where she sat at the kitchen table and couldn't bring herself to go back upstairs, take a shower, get dressed and go to work. And then there had been the many, many days when she couldn't function in the office for more than a few hours before she was exhausted and had to go home. On those nights, she usually curled into a ball and cried herself to sleep. She'd felt it was a necessary part of grieving, to simply give in to the things her mind and body craved, but the reality was that ever since Andrew had come along, those inclinations had started to fade. Just feeling life in the house again made her happy. But once she'd discovered what it meant for that life to be from Andrew, everything had started to change. He was strong and selfless. Warm and caring. Everything she'd always been told he wasn't.

She loved Johnathon, but damn him for portraying his brother in such a negative light.

"Let just say that things have gotten a lot better since you've been here. And not just because you cook for me and make coffee in the morning." She smoothed back his hair. "And it's not because you've done so many things for me around the house or you've listened to my problems or worries. It's because you've never once judged me. Not even for a minute."

"When you've felt the weight of others' judgment, it's hard to want to inflict it on anyone else. Especially someone you care about."

She gazed into his eyes, taking note of the warmth that radiated from the center of her chest. Her heart was putting itself back together, piece by piece, simply because this amazing man had walked into her life at the most inopportune of times. She was falling. She knew it. But she had to be careful. Because she wasn't sure Andrew would ever allow himself to be happy. And that meant she wasn't sure that Andrew would ever stay.

"Will you make me a promise?" she asked.

"What's that?"

"You're already staying for Tara and Grant's wedding. Promise me you'll stay through Christmas."

"Is that what you want?"

She didn't want to think about the alternative. "Yes. Absolutely."

Eleven

Andrew heard Grant's voice plain as day over Miranda's speakerphone. "Can you and Andrew come early today? We have something we need to tell you both."

Miranda cast a curious look at Andrew. They were both still getting dressed for the wedding. And they were already expected to arrive an hour before the rest of the guests. "Is everything okay?" Miranda asked.

"Yes. Everything's fine. But I owe Andrew and you an apology. If you come early, we can set it all straight."

"Okay. We'll be there as soon as we can." Miranda ended the call. "What do you think that's all about?"

"I have no idea, but the thought of an apology sounds pretty good." It sounded better than good, and at least made Andrew slightly more optimistic about attending this wedding. He'd been dreading Grant and Tara's big day. Not because of his date. Going with Miranda was the only reason to put on a tux. But he wasn't thrilled about the idea of facing another virtual firing squad in the form of the bride and groom. It was one thing to be chastised at the Thanksgiving table, and quite another to be given the evil eye over wedding cake and champagne.

"Ready?" he asked Miranda after he'd worked his way into his shoes. "I'm going to save my jacket for after we get there. I don't want it to wrinkle."

Miranda emerged from the closet in her bridesmaid dress, a strapless burgundy gown that nearly made his jaw drop to the floor. "Do I look like a beach ball?"

He went to her, wishing they didn't have to rush out the door. He caressed her silky shoulders. *You look like everything I ever wanted.* "No. You don't. You look absolutely gorgeous and full of life."

"Is that code for beach ball? Because I have to stand next to Astrid, who pretty much has a perfect body and will be wearing the exact same dress. This doesn't bode well for my self-confidence."

"Don't compare yourself to Astrid. You're the most beautiful woman I've ever seen."

She bunched up her lips and narrowed her gaze. "That's not true."

"But it is. Part of that is knowing what's in here." He tapped a finger on her forehead. "And here." He pressed his hand where her heart was, watching as that skeptical look on her face morphed into a smile.

"That's sweet. I don't entirely believe you, but that's okay. You've armed me with enough courage to stand next to Astrid. That's all I needed." Her expression changed again, into one of sheer delight. "Baby's moving," she muttered, reaching for his hand and flattening it against her stomach.

Miranda had told him how active the baby had been, but the movement never seemed to happen when Andrew was around, or when it did, he wasn't able to detect it. He still couldn't feel it now, and he really wanted to. "I just don't feel it."

"A little harder." She pressed his hand even more firmly against her belly.

"I don't want to hurt—" He didn't manage another word before he felt little taps and flutters against his palm. Miranda's pregnancy was mysterious and wondrous, but this was a whole new frontier. Her eyes sparkled when her gaze connected with his. "I feel it," he whispered, dropping his eyes to her belly. "Wow. She's really going for it, isn't she?"

Miranda giggled. "Amazing, isn't it?"

"It really is." He was so in awe that he didn't dare

move until the baby decided to stop making her presence known.

"We should go or we won't be there early at all," she said.

"Okay."

Miranda stopped on her way out of the bedroom to grab her handbag and a wrap for her shoulders from the dresser. Downstairs, they gathered their coats. The ceremony was set to happen in Grant's backyard, which overlooked the Pacific, and although there would be heaters and, later, firepits, it would be chilly by evening.

Outside, they climbed into Miranda's car, with Andrew behind the wheel. She pulled up the address for Grant's house on the GPS. Andrew wasn't entirely sure of the way. As he drove, he could feel his shoulders tighten up. He'd spent so much time worrying about what Grant and Tara would say to him today, that he hadn't taken the time to think about the fact that he hadn't been to a wedding since his fiancée left him. *It's nothing*, he said to himself, but it was eating at him. It was yet another reminder of the many times he'd come up short. Could he ever be enough for Miranda? The fact that he was competing with the memory of Johnathon, the one person he'd always come in second place to, didn't help.

He was in love with her. He couldn't deny himself that label for his feelings, even if he kept it tightly contained in his head and had done so for weeks now, especially since the night they'd made love in her office and had such a heartbreakingly frank conversation. Despite the sensitive subject matter, Miranda brought so much naked honesty to the equation, it stole his breath away. Before he'd met her, Andrew had existed in a world built on fast moves, dubious motives and sleight of hand. Miranda was a complete one-eighty from that, and it fed his soul in a way he hadn't counted on.

He kept looking for moments where he could chalk up his feelings to lust or infatuation, but every time, his thinking led back to one word— *love*. Whenever they were around each other, she'd do or say something that made him want to say it. Even the simplest of smiles from her was enough to make it sit on his lips, but there was always something that made him choke it back.

Victor was the obvious reason. He wouldn't feel right about even broaching the subject until that slate was wiped clean. He needed to fix the problem. But Johnathon was also lurking in the back of his head, telling him that he was treading where he didn't belong.

"Is everything okay?" Miranda asked when they pulled up to Grant's palatial modern home. "You've been quiet."

Now was not the time to unspool everything running circles in his head. "I guess I'm just curious about what Grant has to say to us."

"Nothing else? Because I was thinking about it last night and I have to wonder if it's hard for you to attend a wedding because of your fiancée." Miranda was so in tune with him, it was uncanny. No, she hadn't touched on everything that was bothering him, but she'd keyed in on part of it.

"Maybe a little. I'm fine now. Let's go." He climbed out of the car and helped her with her things.

"Okay. But let me know if you want to talk about it," she said as they walked up the driveway. "Or if it becomes too much. I don't want you to think I'm insensitive by bringing you here."

"Don't worry. I don't."

The front door was wide open, with the occasional person ducking in or out. They stepped inside and asked one of the caterers, "Do you know where Mr. Singleton is?"

"The last time I saw him, he was in his office. Right off the living room. Across from the kitchen."

Miranda and Andrew walked through the wide expanse of the living room, which had been tastefully decorated for the holidays with a tall Christmas tree next to the fireplace, decorated with silver and white ornaments. The house was unbelievable, with stunning views through many windows, all of them leading the eye to the lush landscape and the ocean beyond.

Tara emerged from a door near the back of the house and waved at them. She was wrapped up in a fluffy white robe. "I'm glad you guys are here," she called as she padded toward them in bare feet. "Grant is right in here." She came to a stop outside his office.

Miranda stopped to kiss her on the cheek. "I thought it was bad luck for the groom to see the bride."

"That's just if she's wearing the dress. Hence the robe. Plus, I don't really believe in bad luck. Bad actors, maybe." Tara then turned her attention to Andrew, shocking the hell out of him by offering a hug. "I'm glad you're here."

You are? This was all too bizarre, but Andrew wasn't about to argue. Today was her wedding day. She was entitled to act however she wanted, even if Andrew was thrown for a loop. "I'm happy to be here."

The three stepped inside Grant's home office, tastefully decorated, but it could definitely have benefited from Miranda's deft touch. Grant looked up from his desk, then rounded it to hug Miranda and shake hands with Andrew. He wasn't dressed for the occasion yet, either, wearing jeans and a T-shirt. "Thank you both for coming early. Please. Sit."

This felt a bit like a meeting at Sterling Enterprises, but again, Andrew went with it. He made sure Miranda had her first choice of seating option—the middle of the sofa. He sat next to her while Tara stood next to Grant, the pair holding hands.

"So, I'm sure you're both curious about why we wanted to say this in person, but after everything at Thanksgiving, and then again a few weeks ago in the Sterling offices, Andrew deserves a full-fledged in-person apology. Tara and I are both deeply sorry that we doubted you."

"About Victor?"

"Grant thinks he figured out who he is," Tara said. "His true identity."

Miranda shot a look at Andrew. "Oh, my God. Can you believe this?"

"I'm curious to hear what you learned." Andrew nodded. After all, he'd been the person shouting loudest that Victor was a real person.

"One of the first times Johnathon and I partnered with another developer on a building project, it was with a man named James Bloodworth," Grant started. "This was early days of Sterling Enterprises, after Tara had left the company."

"I remember the Bloodworth fiasco, though," Tara said. "Everyone talked about it."

"Johnathon had been interested in trying a project outside of San Diego, so we partnered with James on a high-rise in Toronto. In short, the deal was a major disaster for him and for Sterling. Everyone lost a pile of money. We underestimated the timeline and the building costs, and we grossly overestimated the market at that time. It was the one and only time we worked outside this city."

"I don't understand. Where does Victor come into this?" Miranda asked, mirroring what Andrew was thinking.

"Victor is James Bloodworth's middle name. Of course, I never knew that," Grant said. "He was terrible to work with. A real hothead. Johnathon and I agreed that we would never partner with him again. At some point, Johnathon went behind my back and cut several deals with him directly, using his own money."

This had been the missing piece of this puzzle—Johnathon's initial partnership with Victor and how Grant could've been left in the dark. Grant did know Victor. The names just weren't right. "This is all starting to make more sense. How did you figure this out?" Andrew had to know how this had come together.

"I've been going through Johnathon's files since his death. Just making sure there wasn't anything crucial tucked away in them. He wasn't always the best at sharing information." Grant cast Tara a knowing smile. "I had a box of them here at the house and Tara needed me to move them into my office for the wedding. I only had one more file to go through, so I did it this morning. It was the last file. Under *V*, for Victor. As near as I can tell, he stopped using his full name after that first failed deal."

Andrew drew a deep breath in through his nose, letting it bring some much-needed oxygen to his brain. Yes, this all made sense, but it was still a lot to take in at one time.

"What does this mean moving forward?" Miranda asked.

"Hopefully, destroying our wedding was the extent of his malicious actions," Tara answered. "We find out who landed the Seaport project on Wednesday, right before Christmas Eve."

What a relief that will be. It almost sounded too good to be true. In fact, Andrew couldn't escape the idea that it likely was. He simply didn't trust Victor to stop or to simply go away. Then again, maybe he was just giving in to old thinking and needed some time to adjust to the idea of not being in constant crisis mode.

Grant extended his hand to Andrew. "I'd like to apologize again. Johnathon definitely left a few surprises behind for us, didn't he?"

Miranda placed her hand on Andrew's knee. "I'm just glad we can all move forward," she said. Her touch was a comfort. It felt like permission to take a deep breath and relax. He hoped he could do that today.

"A wedding seems like a good start," Grant said, taking Tara's hand.

A look of panic crossed Tara's face. "I need to get ready." She shot Miranda a sideways glance. "Do you want to come help me?"

"Sure."

* * *

Miranda knew all along that the situation with Grant, Tara and Andrew had been bothering her, but now that it was resolved, she could hardly believe it. Perhaps that was because Andrew still seemed on edge, forcing smiles and being quiet as she kissed him on the cheek before going to help Tara. "Sit up front. So I can see you."

"I don't feel comfortable doing that. Those seats are for family."

She realized then that she was practically throwing him to the wolves. This wasn't set to be a big wedding, but most guests had known Johnathon, which meant they likely did not have a good opinion of Andrew. "Sit wherever you want. The ceremony will be super short. Then we can spend the rest of the day together."

He unleashed another of those unconvincing smiles. Miranda felt torn between the things she'd promised to Tara, and what she truly wanted to do, which was hold on to Andrew and not let go.

"I will be fine, Miranda. I promise." He pressed a soft kiss to her cheek. "I'll see you after the ceremony."

She admired his strong silhouette as he walked away in the direction of the living room. A heavy sigh came from her lips. She was smitten. But she needed to focus on the task at hand. She turned and rushed down the hall to Grant and Tara's bedroom, where Tara was getting ready.

"If you can just help me get into my dress without getting makeup all over it, that would be great," Tara said.

"Hold on." Astrid slipped into the room, shutting the door behind her. "I'm an expert at this. Let me help." Astrid was a former model. She'd likely done this sort of thing countless times.

"You're here," Miranda said, unable to tear her sights from how incredible Astrid looked in that dress. Andrew's words echoed in her head. *You're the most beautiful woman I've ever seen.* It might not be true, but he at least knew the right thing to say.

"If you could help, that would be amazing," Tara said, easing the robe from her shoulders.

Feeling useless, Miranda stepped aside, leaving Astrid to the job of wrangling the dress. She removed it from the hanger and threaded her arms up through the skirt and bodice, then lifted it above Tara's head. Astrid was tall, and in heels, so she did it with ease. "Raise your arms straight up, but put your chin to your chest," Astrid instructed.

Tara did as she was told. "Won't this mess up my hair?"

"A little. But we'll fix it." Astrid lowered the gown while Tara's torso emerged through the top. Astrid helped her ease the straps over her shoulders, then went to zip her up. "See? No makeup, and your hair looks perfect."

Tara turned around in her dress, a simple but striking winter white satin gown with thin straps, a deep V-neck and a graceful trailing skirt. Astrid and Miranda raced to deliver the good news—she was a beautiful bride.

"It's incredible," Astrid declared.

"Absolutely gorgeous," Miranda added. "Grant's going to flip."

"I'm so glad you're both here. You really are my closest girlfriends. Which is strange, isn't it?"

"I wonder what Johnathon would have thought if he'd ever lived to see this day," Astrid wondered aloud.

"I'm guessing his ego would've been out of control," Tara said. "We look amazing."

Miranda laughed, but she was a little tired of entertaining questions of how Johnathon would've felt about anything. Yes, she'd loved him, but guesses about his wants and desires were looming as too big a presence in all of their lives. "I think it's more important we acknowledge everything the three of us have done to find common ground and work together. It's pretty astounding if you think about it. We could have easily walked out of the lawyer's office after the will was read and gone our separate ways."

"I think that was the money talking," Tara said,

walking over to her bureau and checking her makeup in the mirror hanging over it.

"No. Miranda's right," Astrid said. "The money might have been the starting point, but it was still up to us to keep it all together. That wasn't easy. There were secrets looming and we had to ride it out together." She reached for Miranda's hand and gave it a squeeze. "And now we have a wedding to celebrate, a baby who will be here in a few months and, hopefully, if everything goes right, Sterling Enterprises will win the Seaport contract."

Miranda sighed. It would be nice if that last part happened, but she was also preparing herself for the idea that it might not, and how that might impact Andrew. It could end up being a big blow to his sense of self and the guilt he wrestled with on a daily basis. "Let's all hope for a happy ending."

Astrid's phone beeped with a text. "It's Clay. Grant is down there and Clay is waiting to walk you down the aisle. Delia's with him."

"Sounds like it's game time," Miranda said.

After a last-minute spray of perfume and hairspray for Tara, Miranda checked to make sure the coast was clear in the hall, then they wound around to the back staircase, which led to Grant's lower floor. This house was built into a slight hill, with two thirds of this level still above ground. At the back of the house was a wall of accordion windows that were open today, with the wedding guests in

white wooden folding chairs on the expansive lawn.
Beyond that was the arch, covered in a blanket of
white roses. That had been Miranda's touch. Luck-
ily, Grant had a tall solid wood fence on one side of
his property, which gave them privacy and a break
from the wind.

"Ready?" Clay asked, approaching the three of
them. Delia was holding tight to his hand, but broke
free when she saw Miranda.

Miranda crouched down and kissed her niece on
the head. "You look very pretty in your flower-girl
dress."

"Thank you. These shoes hurt my feet, though."
She rocked one foot from side to side in her white
patent Mary Janes.

"Yeah. I'm afraid that's one of the prices of being
a woman. Wearing shoes that hurt."

"It's time to go," Astrid said. She arranged everyone in order—Delia first, then Miranda, Astrid and
finally Tara on Clay's arm.

Moments later, the music started and Delia did a
wonderful job, tossing flower petals as she started
down the aisle. The guests stood, and that was when
Miranda spotted Andrew, sitting in the second-to-
last row, at the very far end. Would he ever feel a part
of this? She hoped he would. She hoped he would
want to. As she took her turn to march up the aisle,
she stole the chance to lock eyes with him, finding

that familiar mix of sad and tender emotions in his expression.

As promised, the ceremony was short and sweet, and after a rousing round of applause from the attendees and the happy couple's walk down the aisle, the caterers swooped in to rearrange the chairs for the reception as guests left their seats. Miranda found her way to Andrew right away.

"It was nice," he said.

"It was, wasn't it?" She took his hand. "You positive everything is okay?"

He pulled her into his arms and pressed a kiss to the top of her head. "You can stop asking me that. Just enjoy yourself. That's all I really want."

That didn't bring her much comfort or encouragement, but she didn't want to dig deeper. "Let's get you a drink."

"I'll have whatever you're having. I heard something about a spiced Christmas cider."

"You want bourbon in yours?"

He shook his head. "No, thank you."

"You should have a drink if you want one."

"Think of it as a sign of solidarity."

She grinned and popped up onto her toes to kiss his cheek. "You're the best." "I love you" played at her lips, but she didn't want this to be the moment when she blurted it out. She'd wait until she was more sure that there was a chance he would return the feeling. And if that day never came, and he ended up leaving, she'd say it then. Just so he'd never doubt her true feelings. Just so that he could look back on their time together in a happy light. Things between them would never be simple, or cut and dried. Never. He was her dead husband's brother. That was never going away.

They happily made it through dinner and the start of the reception without incident, although Miranda definitely noticed that a few of Johnathon's friends had cast disapproving looks in their direction when she and Andrew were holding hands or dancing. *It's none of their business*, she thought, but she knew it had to bother Andrew. She couldn't shake it off completely herself.

They were in each other's arms on the dance floor when a slow and romantic song segued into a much more raucous one. Guests popped up from their seats and began to move in Miranda and Andrew's direction. She took that as their cue to leave.

"Come on. Let's go steal a minute alone before we sneak out of here." She grabbed his hand and pulled on it.

Andrew took a few steps, but looked out over the party, which was now in full swing. "This is showing signs of lasting all night. Are you sure it's okay if we leave?"

"I'm sure. The cake has been cut. Toasts have been made." She tugged a little harder on his hand.

"I want us to have the moment alone that we didn't really get all day."

He grinned. "I can't deny that's an enticing invitation."

They rushed away from the party, out of the light, and into the deep blue night air. The wind whipped, chilling her face and arms. Miranda had a fleeting thought of a wish for her coat, but she didn't want to ruin the moment. When they got to the farthest reaches of Grant's property, they were less than fifty feet from the precipice, the cliff that overlooked the tumult of the ocean below.

"Come here," Andrew said, pulling her into his arms and wrapping her up in his warmth. She didn't need a coat—all she needed was him. "You're shivering."

"It's okay. I just wanted to soak up this view. With you." She snuggled against his chest and gazed out over the water. The moon, hanging low in the sky, glowed bright, the light glinting off the whitecaps. "Did you enjoy yourself today? I know it couldn't have been easy with so many of Johnathon's friends here."

He tightened his embrace, making her feel like nothing could ever hurt her. She didn't know what she was going to do if he left, but she wasn't going to waste time worrying about what might happen.

"It's not anything I'm not used to, Miranda. I've

spent my entire life contending with my brother. Even in death, he casts a long shadow."

"At some point, you have to find a way to let that fall away. But that's easy for me to say. I've never had to do something like that."

"It's hard when other people foist it upon you. But today was a first step away from that. Tara and Grant finally seeing the light was a good thing."

She eased back her head so she could peer up into his handsome face. She was so glad for a blip of positivity from him. "See? It will just take time."

His hand rose to her cheek, his thumb brushing her skin tenderly. "Speaking of time, I think it's time I get you out of here, into the car and back to a warm house."

"And a warm bed?"

"It will be when we're done with it."

Twelve

On the Monday morning after Grant and Tara's nuptials, Andrew was shaken from his sleep by a terrible thought. He sat up in bed, his breathing labored. What if the wedding cancellation had been a distraction from Victor's true plan to go after Sterling?

"Are you okay?" Miranda muttered, rolling over in bed. "You were talking in your sleep."

Andrew didn't want to share his theory. He wasn't quite awake and hadn't had a chance to think this through. Leaning down, he kissed Miranda's shoulder. "I'm fine. I'll go put on some coffee."

She snuggled her pillow closer. "I'll be down in a little bit. My alarm isn't set to go off for another half hour."

Andrew took his time getting downstairs, thinking through his last conversation with Victor. Victor had suggested that he might interfere with the personal lives of those involved. That explained the problems with the wedding. But it didn't account for the Seaport project, and that was one thing Victor had always fixated on. It was, after all, Johnathon's last chance to be held up as a pillar of his community.

Andrew ground the coffee beans and leaned against the counter as the carafe filled up, drip by drip. The more awake he was, the more likely his idea seemed, but Grant and Tara felt like they were in the home stretch of the Seaport Promenade project. Nothing to worry about. He didn't want to go to them with his theory. It might set them back to right where they'd been before, at war, and with Andrew out in the cold. The person he really needed to broach this with was Clay. But when? It was 7:10 a.m., and Andrew really didn't want Miranda to overhear this conversation with her brother. Hopefully, Clay would understand that Andrew had a good reason for calling.

Clay answered after only one ring. "So I'm not the only one who's an early riser?" he asked.

Andrew managed to grin, despite the worries on his mind. "I don't sleep a lot."

"Me, neither. What's up?"

Andrew could hear Miranda walking around upstairs. She must not have been able to get back to sleep. This would have to be quick. "Can you do me a favor and check in with the city today about the submission for the Seaport?"

"They've made it clear that they don't want us doing that. They're supposed to issue their final decision on Wednesday. December twenty-third."

"I understand, but I'm worried that what Victor pulled with Tara and Grant's wedding was a distraction. It forced everyone, especially Tara and Grant, to focus on things other than work over the last two weeks." Andrew really hoped that this conjecture would all end up being nothing. "This is just a precaution. You guys are so close to the finish line. I'd hate for anything to mess that up."

"Okay. Sure thing. I'll do it as soon as I get into the office."

Andrew heard Miranda's footsteps on the stairs. "Let me know what you learn."

"Will do."

Andrew ended the call and tucked his phone into the back pocket of his pajama pants just as Miranda was walking into the room. Seeing her always brought up a firestorm of feelings. He was tired of living on this edge, where he was in her life but not all the way in. Where his affection for her had been expressed physically, but never in words. He wanted to put everything on the line, but he was terrified of where it would leave Miranda. If he ended up going back to Seattle, he had to know that she'd be okay. That he hadn't made everything she'd been through so much worse, by stirring up trouble and leaving it unresolved.

"Coffee?" he asked.

"Please. You know how I feel about Mondays."

He poured her a cup of coffee, adding a healthy splash of cream. "I'm hoping this will make it ever so slightly better."

"Exactly the way I like it." She took a sip, then smiled warmly at him.

Moments like this really got to him—the seemingly insignificant glimpses of everyday life. He couldn't fathom leaving San Diego once everything with Victor was resolved. *If it's resolved*, he reminded himself. The reality was that he wouldn't feel good about professing his feelings, or his desire to stay, until he had redeemed himself. Grant and Tara's forgiveness had been a big step forward, but he wanted a clean slate. Miranda deserved a fresh start that came without conditions.

"I've decided not to go into the office for the rest of the week after today." Miranda reached for his hand. "It'll give us some time together. A few days before Christmas to relax."

Andrew hadn't wanted anything so badly, ever. "Great."

"I ordered some artwork for the nursery a month or so ago. It's due to arrive tomorrow. We could hang that. Maybe watch a Christmas movie." She shrugged. "I don't know. That probably sounds pretty unexciting."

It sounds like everything I ever wanted. "I'm sure it'll be more fun than work."

"That reminds me. I need to check my email. There's a chance my only client meeting today is going to be moved up. I'll be right back." She traipsed off into the living room, presumably heading for her office.

Andrew went to work on breakfast—some eggs, sausage and fresh fruit—and tried to clear his head. There was a distinct chance that everything was fine—Clay might very well call him sometime after nine and proclaim that all was good with Sterling's place in the final round for the Seaport project. Miranda would come home after work and he'd make a fabulous meal for her. Hopefully, they'd make love and he'd hold her in his arms while she slept. They'd spend several days together, tucked away in this house, and ultimately spend a beautiful holiday together. His first truly happy Christmas.

If all of that could happen, it might be the right time to tell her his true feelings. He'd put it all on the line. And if he was fortunate, Miranda would say that she felt the same way. Could he be that lucky? He wanted to believe he was due, but he was smart enough to know that the world didn't always work like that.

Miranda joined him in the kitchen and they sat down to breakfast together.

With her first bite, Miranda moaned. "You're spoiling me." She always expressed her sincere appreciation for his cooking skills, and this morning was no different.

He soaked up every second of the attention. "Not possible."

She grinned. "I like watching you try."

And I love trying. After breakfast was done, Miranda went up to shower while Andrew cleaned up the kitchen and prayed that his phone would ring soon. It didn't happen before Miranda was out the door for work, so Andrew got cleaned up and dressed for the day.

The caller ID lit up with Clay's information a little after ten. "You were right. Our bid has been withdrawn. Completely taken out of the running."

Andrew's heart began to hammer. He took no pleasure in seeing his hunch proven right. "What happened?"

"Apparently, a woman with a letter on Sterling Enterprises letterhead showed up at the planning office on Friday morning. It was a formal request to withdraw from the competition."

"The day before the wedding."

"Yes. Grant and Tara weren't in the office at all that day. And neither was I because they had the

Christmas pageant at Delia's school that morning, then I went with Grant to pick up their rings."

"Can you undo what's been done?" Andrew's mind was running a million miles a minute as he thought about what his next move might be.

"Yes. We've already begun the process. The clerk was annoyed at first, but I think I sweet-talked her. That's not really my forte, but I think we're going to be okay."

Finally, Andrew could exhale. Clay had set things back on track from the Sterling side of things. Still, this had been entirely too close a call. Andrew needed Sterling to get across the finish line on Wednesday. They might not win the bid, but at least it would be because everything had played out the way it was supposed to. "Okay. I'm going to get to work on tracking down Victor and finally putting an end to this."

"Andrew, you know I believe in you, but I've heard you say that so many times. What's different today?"

All Andrew could think about was the prospect of spending the next few days with Miranda. Beyond that, maybe more? It felt like his future was lying at his feet, but he was going to have to wrap it all up. He had to redeem himself. "I have an idea."

"Maybe there's just no stopping this guy and we have to ride it out until he gets bored and walks away."

"I've thought about that, but I don't want us all existing under this dark cloud. It's no way to live."

"Us all? That almost makes it sound like you're planning on staying. Have you and Miranda talked about this?"

Andrew hoped he wasn't overstepping. "We haven't. I haven't felt right about saying anything until the Victor situation is resolved."

"But you want to stay?"

"How would it make you feel if I said yes?" Andrew wanted to believe that he and Clay were close now, that it was okay for him to ask this question, but he wasn't sure.

"I'd say that it's an amazing idea."

Andrew couldn't contain the smile that crossed his face. "Good. Just don't tell your sister. I'm not going to bring it up until this is all put to bed."

"Don't worry about me. Mum's the word."

Andrew's phone beeped with another call. It was an unknown caller, but Andrew had an irrational hope that it might be Victor. "Clay, I need to go. Keep me posted if anything changes."

"I will." Andrew hung up and answered the other call. "Hello?"

"Mr. Sterling?"

Andrew was shocked as hell. "Sandy, are you okay? You sound terrible."

"Were you serious about the offer you made me before?"

"Of course I was. Why? Are you thinking about flipping on Victor?"

"He just called me. He's enraged. Someone at Sterling called the city and got them to put Sterling back into the bidding process. He thought he'd successfully pulled the company out of the running."

Andrew didn't want to tip his hand. He had little faith in the idea of trusting Sandy. "Oh, wow. I didn't know."

"He's furious."

Andrew's stomach soured. "Look, Sandy. I'm happy to give you what I promised you, but at this point, I'm not sure you can help me. It sounds like Victor's going to forge ahead, with or without you."

"I have something that can help you take him down. Audio recordings."

"Of what?"

"Every conversation he and I ever had. Everything he ever asked me to do. And it's not just the Sterling Enterprises plan. Victor had me doing other corporate espionage. Scary stuff with very big players."

Andrew's thoughts were moving fast. "Will you give them to me? My offer still stands if you will. Five million."

"The money's not enough anymore. I need to disappear. I need to get to somewhere where he'll never find me. I know too much and if the recordings come out, he'll know that I double-crossed him."

"One of my private planes is in a hangar down

at Gray Municipal. I can get you to Mexico. Pietro, my security chief, can go with you. Once you're in a safe place, you give us the audio recordings and we'll transfer the money."

"I want *you* to do it. I want you to come with me."

"What? Why?"

"Because I trust you more than I trust Pietro. You have more to lose. You're the one who's been chasing Victor this whole time."

Andrew's thoughts hung on Sandy's words. He *did* have everything to lose. If this all went down the drain with Sterling, the company would ultimately be fine. They'd find a way to move forward, make millions and Johnathon's reputation would most likely remain intact. Yes, they would suffer the embarrassment of not landing the massive public contract they were expected to win. Miranda might ultimately forgive Andrew for things he'd done. But he would not have made peace with his brother's memory, and he would never feel right with the world until he did that. He had to know deep in his heart that he'd done everything possible to save what Johnathon had built. "Okay. I'll take you."

"I don't want you to just fly me over the border and drop me off. I need you to take me somewhere remote. Somewhere that's safe."

Andrew had traveled all over the world, but one locale he'd visited years ago had struck him as the perfect place to disappear—a tiny village tucked away in the mountains of Costa Rica. "I have an idea. I can tell you on the plane. Ping me your location? I'll pick you up myself."

"Okay. Please hurry."

Andrew ended the call and rushed upstairs. He did not want to leave, but what choice did he have? He'd put Sandy in this situation at the very beginning. Yes, it had been her choice to side with Victor, but he couldn't blame other people for their poor choices. He'd made too many of his own.

Upstairs, he called Clay, and put him on speakerphone while he packed up the suitcase he'd wheeled into this house weeks ago.

"Hey, Andrew. What's up?" Clay asked.

"I need you to keep an eye on your sister for the next few days."

"Going somewhere?"

"Yes. I need to take care of our big problem. I think it's best if I don't tell you where. No idea who might be listening."

"Is Miranda in danger?"

"No. I'll have my head of security stay in San Diego. We'll have someone with eyes on the house the whole time, but I'd feel better if you were checking in with her, too." Andrew's phone screen flashed a notification from the number Sandy had called from. It was her location. "I have to go. I don't plan on checking in. I don't want to leave any lines of communication open, okay?"

"Got it. Good luck."

Andrew zipped his bag shut and thundered down the stairs, but he came to a stop when he saw the array of beautiful holiday decorations in the living room. The fireplace mantel had the lovely scene Miranda had designed—with pine boughs, red velvet ribbon and twinkly white lights. Over the doorway into the foyer was what Andrew now knew was a swag, of silver Christmas bells in various sizes and glittery garland, all artfully arranged. In the corner sat the Christmas tree, looking like something out of a magazine, with its array of carefully chosen ornaments. These things had brought Christmas spirit with Miranda's skilled guidance, but she was what made those warm feelings come to life. He hated the thought of missing out on the next few days with her. He was supposed to be here. They'd made plans. He intended to return, but he'd had so many intentions over the years that hadn't turned out. He really hoped that wouldn't be the case this time. Regardless, it was time to let her know he wouldn't be here when she arrived home from work.

He waited until he was pulling his car out of Miranda's driveway to make the call.

"I feel like I just saw you," Miranda answered. "Are you sure you're okay?"

"I am, but I have to leave town for a few days."

"Wait. What's wrong?"

The distress in her voice made his task that much

more difficult. "I'm within striking distance of fixing my problem."

"Victor? Seriously? I thought that was over."

"It's not. Not completely, at least."

"This is starting to feel like a wild-goose chase. Is this really necessary? Can't someone else deal with him?"

"I started this. I have to finish it."

Miranda grumbled. "You don't have to. You've tried everything imaginable. You're the only one expecting this of yourself. You hold yourself to a standard that's impossible to meet."

He knew he was being stubborn. It didn't change his determination to follow through. "I know."

"Just this morning, we talked about spending the next few days together. You said it sounded like fun. That's not enough to make you stay?"

"Don't make this harder than it already is, okay?"

Miranda didn't immediately say anything in return, but he could hear her breathing. "You're definitely coming back?"

"That's my plan. Yes."

"When?"

Andrew didn't want to give definitive answers, but he also didn't want to leave her hanging. He'd already saddled her with so much uncertainty over the last month or so. "I'll be back by Christmas, okay? I promise." He hoped like hell that nothing bad happened and that he didn't have to break that promise. It would crush her visions of a happy holiday.

"Will you also promise me that you'll be careful?" Her voice was starting to crack.

"Of course."

"Because I want you to come back, Andrew. I hope you know that."

He managed half a smile, but his heart was aching. There were so many things he wanted to say, but once again he was overwhelmed by the need to wait until the time was right. "I want to come back. I hope *you* know that."

"Okay. 'Bye. Be careful."

"Goodbye, Miranda." He hit the red button to end the call before he could say what he longed to tell her… *I love you.*

Thirteen

By late afternoon on Wednesday evening, Miranda was starting to lose hope. Andrew had been gone more than forty-eight hours. Where was he and what could he possibly be doing? She picked up her phone and pulled up his number in her contacts. It rang and rang, as it had the other times she'd called since he'd left on Monday. It then went to his voice mail, just like before. The sound of his voice made her ache for his presence. *"This is Andrew Sterling. Please leave a message."*

"Hey. It's me. I'm just calling because I'm worried and this makes me feel better. Please call or text me to let me know that you're okay. Even just a thumbs-up emoji would be a big help." She ended the call and tossed her phone to the other end of the couch. She was tired of feeling so helpless. The last time she'd felt like this was during the first month after Johnathon's death, when she'd had to get used to being all alone in this big house. In some ways, she felt as though she was reliving that loss. It wasn't a pleasant feeling.

Her phone rang and she scrambled, crawling on hands and knees across the cushions and grabbing it without looking at the caller ID. "Hello? Andrew?"

"Sorry to disappoint. It's Tara."

Miranda slumped back against a pile of throw pillows, her heart practically in her throat. "Oh, it's okay. What's up?"

"The city just made the announcement. Sterling landed the Seaport project."

Miranda struggled to understand why her first reaction was tears. Perhaps it was stress. Perhaps it was closing this chapter when Andrew wasn't around. Sterling had made it through despite Victor's interference. If Johnathon was still here, he would've been so pleased. "Congratulations. You all must be so excited."

"Everyone is. There's a fair bit of relief, too."

"How are you going to celebrate?"

"We'll do it in January. After the holidays. After pulling a wedding together in two weeks, I'm trying to take a break from party planning."

"Makes perfect sense."

Tara hesitated on the line, which made Miranda wonder if there was more she wanted to say. "I take it you haven't heard from Andrew?"

"You know that he left?"

"Yes. Clay told Grant and me. Don't worry. We haven't told anyone."

"Okay."

"I'll be honest. I'm worried. Grant and I wanted him to take care of the situation with Victor, but from a distance. We never thought he'd get on a plane and go after him."

Miranda felt her blood go cold. Yes, she'd believed Andrew all this time, but it somehow made it worse that everyone else now knew that Victor was real. "Do you think he's in danger? No one has heard from him since Monday afternoon. I don't even know what to do now. I'm so consumed with worry."

"Do you want Grant to do some asking around? See what we can find out?"

All Miranda could think about was that Andrew had wanted this all kept quiet. "No. I don't want any of us to do anything to jeopardize his safety." Speaking of which, Miranda probably needed to stop leaving him messages. There was no telling what sort of circumstances he was in.

"Okay. Will you please call us when you hear from him? Andrew was right all along, and Grant and I will never stop feeling bad about it. We also feel indebted to him. His quick thinking on Monday morning kept us in the game. We got the Seaport project. Everyone gets their happy ending."

Except me. Miranda hated that her mind would go to such a negative place, but she couldn't help it. "I'm so glad. Hopefully I'll get to tell him soon."

"Please keep us posted."

"I will. 'Bye, Tara."

"Goodbye."

Miranda hung up. All this good news and it still didn't make her feel any better.

She worried that the obvious was staring her in the face—Andrew might not come back. She had to distract herself, so she went into the kitchen and made herself a mug of cocoa, then settled on the sofa to watch a movie. *It's a Wonderful Life* was on the TV, and it had just started, showing snowy scenes in black-and-white of quaint Bedford Falls. Miranda turned the volume low. The movie was so familiar, she could recite nearly every line, but she couldn't focus enough to watch it. Maybe Andrew was going back to Seattle and he simply couldn't bring himself to tell her.

That would've been the Andrew of old, the fictional one constructed by Johnathon and sometimes Grant and Tara. Miranda knew that wasn't the real Andrew. The real Andrew kept his promises. He made good on everything he said he'd do. As night fell and the clock ticked closer to Christmas Eve, she continued to waver between hope and disappointment. He'd said he'd be back in time for Christmas. There weren't many hours left until Christmas Eve would be upon them. The thought of him not showing up, in time or at all, reminded her of the many times she'd defended him. She'd always wanted to believe that he would never lead her astray or let her down. Although he'd always been thankful to have her confidence, he'd also told her that she didn't need to do it. It had always been a gut instinct. A reflex.

This was her connection to Andrew—immediate and visceral. Something she couldn't explain. They'd had an invisible bond from the moment they met. Yes, it all started with Johnathon, and that fact still ate at her from time to time. How she wished she could talk to her dead husband, explain to him that her feelings for Andrew didn't mean that she wouldn't always love him. When the baby arrived, that feeling would likely grow. But Miranda had a big heart, one meant for giving, and also receiving. She hadn't planned it, but she'd fallen. In love. With his brother. And she should have been smarter about it. She should have told him before he took off.

Miranda's phone rang. She jumped just as she had every other time over the last two days. She fought the disappointment when, once again, it wasn't Andrew. She loved talking to her brother, but it wasn't quite the same.

"You don't have to keep checking up on me," she said without offering a hello.

"Oh, but I do. I promised Andrew. Why don't you come over and hang out with us? Delia would love to see you. We're baking Christmas cookies. I'll come and pick you up."

"I think I'll stay put. Thank you, though." The invitation truly sounded lovely and she sure could have used the distraction, but she wanted to hold on to hope, even when she wondered if her optimism wasn't about to bite her on the butt. Sometimes things didn't turn out okay. "I talked to Tara a little while ago. Congratulations on the Seaport project."

"Thanks, but it's not really my victory. It was the whole team. And frankly, it was the wives. You three were the ones who pushed the hardest."

"I guess we did."

"You sound tired."

"I am. Although I don't know why. I've basically been puttering around the house for two days. I haven't done much more than worry."

"That can be draining in its own right," Clay said.

"I suppose." Miranda took another sip of her cocoa and set the mug on the end table. "You haven't heard from him, have you?"

"You know I would've called you right away if I had, right?"

"I know." Of course she did. It still didn't hurt to ask. "I think I'm going to go to bed."

"It's so early," Clay noted.

"I know. I'm super tired."

"Okay. We'll see you on Christmas morning for brunch at our place?"

"Absolutely."

"Sleep well."

Miranda didn't have the energy to walk all the way upstairs. She clicked off the TV, grabbed a throw blanket from the end of the sofa and arranged a few pillows until she was comfortable. She tried to think good thoughts as she closed her eyes and felt her body slowly giving in to sleep. How she hoped she wouldn't be spending this Christmas alone. How she hoped she wouldn't have to face her future without the man she loved.

Andrew's plane touched down on the private landing strip at the San Diego airport, smooth as silk. He took his new phone off airplane mode. His old one had died an untimely death in Costa Rica, falling out of his pocket and into the small plunge pool of the cottage he'd found for Sandy. He still didn't have the message he'd been waiting for from Pietro. He wasn't going to tell Miranda that the coast was clear until he was absolutely certain that was the truth.

He'd left his rental down at Gray Municipal when he'd left town with Sandy, so he had a driver pick him up. "Mr. Sterling. I believe you're expecting this." The driver handed over a small black velvet box as he held the door.

Andrew popped it open. It was exactly as he'd

remembered, even though he hadn't looked at it in years. "Thank you." He dropped it into his pocket and climbed inside the car. Excitement bubbled up in his body at the thought of seeing Miranda. He was nervous, too. He could imagine relief at confessing his feelings, but he could also picture several different types of rejection. She might want to wait. It was awfully soon. Her husband hadn't been gone very long.

Finally, Andrew's phone buzzed in his hand. It was Pietro. "Well?" Andrew asked when he answered.

"I'm sorry I'm a little late in calling you. His flight was delayed, but he's off to Munich. I watched the plane take off myself." Andrew had instructed Pietro to buy a ticket for the flight, just so he could accompany Victor through security and down to the gate.

Andrew had never breathed such a big sigh of relief. He had a promise from Victor that he would stay in Europe for the next twelve months. Andrew had plenty of insurance to make sure Victor would keep a safe distance. Forever. "Thank you so much. I couldn't have done this without you."

"Are you on your way to Ms. Sterling's?"

"I am."

"Good luck," Pietro said with a glint of mischief in his voice.

"Thank you for having one of your guys track

down the ring in Seattle and sending it down. I just got it."

"No trouble at all, sir. Is there anything else I can do for you?"

"Now that we have everything wrapped up, you and your guys are welcome to head back to Seattle."

"And what are your plans?" Pietro asked.

"I don't know. But I'm hoping that I get to stay here in San Diego."

"If you do, what does that mean for your operation in Seattle?"

"I don't know, exactly, but I do know that you'll always have a job. Don't worry about that."

"Good to know, sir. I can't imagine working for anyone else."

Andrew smiled. "Good. And good night, Pietro. Job well done."

"Good night, sir."

Andrew hung up the phone. That call from Pietro had been the last thing he was waiting on before he called Miranda. They were only ten minutes from her house, but he didn't want to hold out for even a second more. Unfortunately, the call went to her voice mail. Was she in bed already? It was only nine-thirty. None of that made sense. Hopefully, everything could be cleared up once he arrived.

As soon as they arrived at Miranda's, Andrew grabbed his suitcase and beelined for the front door, then put in the security code for the electronic lock.

Inside, the house was so quiet. "Miranda?" he asked, setting down his bag. There was no answer.

He spotted a soft ray of light beaming into the hall from the living room. He went to investigate, and spotted Miranda all curled up on the sofa, asleep. He crept closer, finding emotion welling up inside him. She was everything. His whole world. And he'd been tormenting himself, waiting to tell her.

He kneeled down next to the couch and stole a moment to look at how truly beautiful she was in serene slumber. Her amazing mouth was slack, her eyelids pale and her lashes dark against her skin. Her gorgeous hair tumbled across her shoulders. He braced himself by placing a hand on her upper arm and leaning in to kiss her on her forehead. "Miranda?" he whispered as he moved back.

Her eyes drifted halfway, then suddenly popped open. The look of surprise on her face made him wonder if he'd scared her. "Oh, my God. You're here."

He sat back as she pushed herself to sitting then lunged for him. They landed in a heap on the floor. She kissed him at least ten times. Maybe more. All he could think was that if this was his reward for all of the pain and misery he'd been through, it was absolutely worth it.

"You're back. You're here. I was so worried."

"I'm sorry I didn't call. My phone died and it took some time to get a new one in Costa Rica."

"That's where you went?"

He nodded but held his finger to his lips. "Yes. But we can't tell anyone. That's where Sandy is. I got her relocated. It took some doing with setting up offshore accounts and getting her into the country in the first place. But she's good. She should be safe. From Victor."

"Sterling got the Seaport contract. Tara called me earlier today."

"I heard."

"Does that mean Victor is gone? For good?" Andrew was going to spare Miranda the details, but it was safe to say that Victor would not be coming back. Andrew had hours of audio of Victor detailing his various schemes, most of which were illegal. Andrew's only ask for not handing them over to some of Victor's more notorious partners was that Victor disappear.

"He is. He's gone, darling. Nobody has to worry about him anymore."

Miranda sat up, her legs curled up under her body. "Darling? You've never called me a pet name before."

Andrew pushed himself to sitting. "Huh. I guess I haven't."

She smiled wide. "I like it a lot."

His heart began to hammer again. "Good. Because I need to ask you something."

She shook her head. "No. Hold on. There's one thing I need to tell you first. If that's okay."

He laughed quietly. She was so adorable when she was being pushy. "Of course. Whatever you want."

"I realized when you were gone how much I need you. And how many things I left unsaid while you were here. About what you mean to me. About the void you've filled in my—"

He shook his head wildly. "Hold on. I feel the same way, Miranda."

A tear rolled down her cheek. "Can I finish? Please? I've got this all rehearsed in my head and I don't want to forget a word of it."

"Yes. Of course." How could he say no when she was crying?

"I can't lose another person in my life, Andrew. I can't lose you."

"I love you," he blurted. "I'm sorry. I couldn't wait anymore."

Now the tears were rolling down her cheeks even faster. "You do? Because I love you, too. Please tell me you won't leave."

"Please tell me I can stay."

She nodded and he slipped his hands into her silky hair, pulling her face to his. They drifted into the kiss and Andrew let fanciful thoughts swirl in his head, even when he was normally not inclined to give in to such things. This felt like the start. A fresh one. Full of bright promise. Even with everything that had gone wrong in his life, he still felt lucky. He had love and good fortune. He was about to have a family if she answered his question the way he hoped she would.

He reared back his head and pulled the box out of his pocket, opening it for Miranda. "Will you marry me, Miranda? Will you be my wife?"

He wasn't sure exactly what her reaction would be, but he hadn't expected how eagerly she would wipe away her tears and thrust her left hand forward. "Oh, my God. Yes. I would love to marry you."

Andrew removed the ring from its safe spot and slipped it onto Miranda's finger. "It was my mom's, and it belonged to my dad's mom before that. It's quite literally the only Sterling family heirloom that exists. I had Pietro get it from Seattle while I was getting Sandy settled."

"You did that? For me?" She admired the ring with a flutter of her lovely fingers.

"Do you like it? Be honest. You can tell me if you don't."

"I love it. I absolutely love it. It's beautiful. It has so much character."

"Good. Because the other person I tried to give it to thought it was ugly and wanted something else."

"That should've been your first sign."

She might be right. "Probably."

Her gaze returned to his face. "I know this couldn't have been easy. Proposing a second time in your life."

A breathy laugh escaped his lips. "You want to

know what's funny? I never even thought about that. I was nervous, but only because it was you. I wasn't anxious about the actual question."

"Why would I make you nervous? We've grown so close. You can tell me anything at all. I will not judge you."

"It's precisely that. You always believe in me. Even when you had reason to not feel that way. I worry a bit that I'm not worthy, but I think that's normal. You are pretty amazing."

"You're the one who's amazing." She leaned closer and gave him a soft kiss that warmed him from head to toe.

He couldn't wait to get her upstairs. He got up from the floor and reached down for her hand. "Come on. Time for bed."

"Sleeping or bed?"

He laughed and gently pulled her along toward the stairs. "Bed, if that's okay with you. I want to make love to my fiancée."

Miranda stopped before they started their ascent. "I'm so excited you made it back in time for Christmas."

"I told you I'd be back. I wouldn't have missed it for the whole world."

"I can't wait to subject you to all of my favorite Christmas Eve traditions tomorrow. Baking cookies. Lighting a fire. Listening to Christmas music."

He wasn't sure what to say. What sort of words match the moment when you realize you have it all?

"I'm sure it sounds like a lot," she said.

He didn't hesitate. He swept her into his arms and started up the stairs. "Honestly, it sounds like all I ever wanted."

Epilogue

Four months later

Baby Chloe was crying. Miranda knew it was just a ploy, but she watched as Andrew totally fell for it.

"Shh. Shh. It's okay." He scooped her up out of the baby carrier and gently placed her over his shoulder. "There's no need to cry."

"You don't have to pick her up every time she cries, you know." Miranda walked up behind him and lowered her head to get the baby's attention. Chloe's eyes lit up and she unleashed her new, tooth-less grin when she spotted her mom. Miranda's heart swelled to twice its size. This was a regular occurrence. It happened several hundred times a day, especially since Chloe started to smile a few weeks ago.

"It kills me when she cries. I can't help it." Andrew turned so he could look Miranda in the eye. Damn, he was sexy with a baby in his arms. "You can tell me to stop it, but I doubt I ever will."

"I forgive you. I just don't want her to get spoiled." Miranda glanced at the clock on the wall. "Oh, shoot. We'd better pack up the car or we're going to be late."

Andrew grabbed the diaper bag from the kitchen counter and began sifting through it with Chloe still in his arms. "Plenty of diapers. Change of clothes. Wipes. Pacifier. Oh, no." He turned to Miranda. "Where's her inchworm?"

Chloe had a stuffed inchworm sewn of soft fabric in a rainbow of colors. It was small enough for her to wrap her tiny fingers around and hold on to it. "I think it's on the sofa."

"I'll get it."

"I can do it," she said. "You can put her in her carrier."

"I'd rather wait until the last second. She's just going to start crying."

Miranda shook her head, grabbed the diaper bag and walked around to the other side of the couch, finding the inchworm. "This is the last second. Tara will be furious if we're late."

"So much buildup to this thing. You'd think someone was getting married or having a baby." He nestled Chloe into her seat, and sure enough, she started to wail the second he had her strapped in. "We'd better hurry up."

They hustled out to the car and Andrew clicked the carrier into its base in the back seat of Miranda's SUV. He rushed to start the car. As soon as the engine rumbled to life, Chloe stopped crying. He was visibly relieved. "Next stop, Seaport Promenade?"

"Hard to believe the day has finally come to break ground on this thing. I don't know about you, but I'm relieved. And ready to stop hearing about it."

"I swear it's all anyone talks about lately," Andrew said.

Of course, Miranda knew very well that Andrew was relieved. In many ways, today was about him facing Johnathon one more time, but this time, he was armed with vindication and the knowledge that he'd done right by everyone, even himself. Johnathon's legacy would be sealed, but Andrew had a life ahead of him with Miranda and Chloe. It didn't need to be said that Andrew knew he was the lucky one, after a lifetime of feeling like he'd been on the losing end of that relationship.

They arrived downtown a few minutes later and Andrew found a spot near the convention center, which meant a short walk to the promenade. He unloaded Chloe's stroller and tossed the diaper bag into the storage basket while Miranda put in her seat. They were a well-oiled machine by now, nearly two months after Chloe's arrival, but it hadn't always been like this. The first three or four weeks were rocky, all three of them operating on too little sleep because Chloe had been colicky. She'd arrived on February fourth, so at that point, Miranda and Andrew were still in the honeymoon phase of their relationship, even though they hadn't yet tied the knot. There was nothing like sleepless nights and too few showers to test a partnership. But they got through it and Andrew took to parenthood like a fish to water. He might be strong, and sometimes stolid, but he'd been putty in Chloe's hand from the minute he laid eyes on her in the delivery room, and they both cried their eyes out at the miracle before them. It still felt like a dream some days. A beautiful, perfect dream.

They strolled down the sidewalk, enjoying the warmth of this sunny April day. They reached a break in the city buildings, one of the walkways to the place where the old Seaport development had once been. The demolition began in January, right after Sterling landed the project, and was completed in short order. Included in that was the destruction of the wedding pavilion, the one where Andrew would've gotten married if his fiancée hadn't left him. Andrew had a bit of an epiphany that day, wondering aloud if perhaps Johnathon hadn't had nefarious intent when he'd wanted to pursue the Seaport. Maybe he'd wanted to see it erased and brought back to life in a new form, one that wouldn't have to cause

Andrew so much pain. It was a lovely thought, and although no one had any way of knowing, he and Miranda had decided that would be the story they would tell the baby. For Johnathon's many faults and missteps, he had been a good man with a big heart. And he'd been part of bringing the two most important people in Miranda's life, Chloe and Andrew, to her.

When they emerged on the other side of the buildings, they spotted the construction site, ringed in chain-link fence with an enormous sign that read Sterling and Singleton Enterprises. That was another development since Christmas—in February, soon after the baby was born, Grant invited Andrew to merge his development firm with Sterling Enterprises. It was a natural pairing, plus Andrew wasn't going anywhere and it seemed foolish of him to branch out into San Diego development and attempt to compete with the company his brother had started.

In turn, Andrew felt it was only right that Grant's last name finally go on the company letterhead. Andrew kept the Seattle office open, but only went up once a month or so, and only overnight. He never wanted to be far away from San Diego or Miranda and the baby. *I need my family*, he'd say whenever he decided that he couldn't bring himself to be gone for more than twenty-four hours.

There was a small crowd assembled, upwards of fifty people, most of them Sterling-Singleton employees or the press. To the far side stood Astrid and Clay. They were in the midst of planning their wedding, which was set for June on the beach in Coronado. They'd wanted to wait until Delia was out of school so they could take her to Norway for a month and introduce her to Astrid's homeland. Miranda had never seen her brother happier, and that, in turn, made her own happiness that much brighter and more complete.

"Hey there," Clay said, when Andrew and Miranda rolled up with the stroller. "Where's my beautiful niece?"

Andrew pulled back the sunshade a fraction of an inch and peered inside. "She's sleeping."

"Well, can I see her?" Clay asked.

Miranda and Astrid laughed, hugging each other. "They're so funny," Astrid said.

"That's one word for it," Miranda added.

"Folks, we're ready to start," Tara's voice announced over a loudspeaker. She and Grant were both standing with hardhats on and shovels in their hands. Alongside them were the mayor and several members of the city council. Andrew had been invited to participate in this part of things, but he'd decided against it. Andrew said it didn't matter that he was the Sterling part of the company name now. He'd rather stand with his family.

"We'll keep this short so everyone can enjoy this

beautiful day," Tara continued. "With that, I'll turn it over to Grant Singleton to make the dedication."

Grant took the microphone from his wife and kissed her on the cheek. "Sterling Enterprises has been fortunate to be a part of this community for more than fifteen years, but it's always been in the private sector. Yes, we've built some beautiful, state-of-the-art buildings in this city, but this project is the one that will ultimately mean the most. It is my sincere hope that this will be a place for the citizens who live here, and those who travel to visit our amazing city, to gather for years to come. And with that, let us break ground."

Grant, Tara and several members of the city council poised their shovels in the artfully arranged mound of dirt at the entrance to the construction site. After a count to three, they all dug in, officially breaking ground on the redevelopment of the Seaport Promenade.

The crowd erupted in applause, which noticeably put Andrew on edge. He peeked inside Chloe's stroller to check on her. "Okay. Good. She's still asleep."

Miranda laughed quietly, then leaned in for a kiss. "I love you, Andrew."

"I love you, too."

They both looked on as Grant, Tara and the other local dignitaries shook hands. "You know, I've been thinking," Andrew said. "What if we got married here? When it's all done?"

That was the one piece of their happy ending that hadn't happened yet. Miranda hadn't wanted to walk down the aisle at eight or nine months pregnant, and they were still adjusting to Chloe's arrival. Ahead of them was Clay and Astrid's wedding. Perhaps Christmas would work well. It *was* Miranda's favorite time of year.

"Really? You want to do that?" she asked. "This place holds some bad memories, doesn't it?"

He shook his head and looked over at her, shielding his eyes. "Miranda, darling, you need to know something."

"What's that?"

"With you in my life, there are no more bad memories. Only happy ones."

* * * * *

*Don't miss the other two romances in
Karen Booth's exciting miniseries,
The Sterling Wives:*

Once Forbidden, Twice Tempted
High Society Secrets

Available from Harlequin Desire!

WE HOPE YOU ENJOYED THIS BOOK FROM

Luxury, scandal, desire—welcome to the lives of the American elite.

Be transported to the worlds of oil barons, family dynasties, moguls and celebrities. Get ready for juicy plot twists, delicious sensuality and intriguing scandal.

6 NEW BOOKS AVAILABLE EVERY MONTH!

COMING NEXT MONTH FROM

DESIRE

Available December 1, 2020

#2773 THE WIFE HE NEEDS
Westmoreland Legacy: The Outlaws • by Brenda Jackson
Looking to settle down, Alaskan CEO Garth Outlaw thinks he wants
a convenient bride. What he doesn't know is that his pilot,
Regan Fairchild, wants *him*. Now, with two accidental weeks together in
paradise, will the wife he needs be closer than he realized?

#2774 TEMPTED BY THE BOSS
Texas Cattleman's Club: Rags to Riches • by Jules Bennett
The only way to get Kelly Prentiss's irresistible workaholic boss
Luke Holloway to relax is to trick him—into taking a vacation with her!
The island heat ignites a passion they can't ignore, but will it be back to
business once their getaway ends?

#2775 OFF LIMITS ATTRACTION
The Heirs of Hansol • by Jayci Lee
Ambitious Colin Song wants his revenge—by working with producer
Jihae Park. But remaining enemies is a losing battle with their sizzling
chemistry! Yet how can they have a picture-perfect ending when
everyone's secret motives come to light?

#2776 HOT HOLIDAY FLING
by Joss Wood
Burned before, the only thing businessman Hunt Sheridan wants is
a no-strings affair with career-focused Adie Ashby-Tate. When he
suggests a Christmas fling, it's an offer she can't refuse. But will their hot
holiday fantasy turn into a gift neither was expecting?

#2777 SEDUCING THE LOST HEIR
Clashing Birthrights • by Yvonne Lindsay
When identical twin Logan Harper learns he was stolen at birth, he vows
to claim the life he was denied. Until he's mistakenly seduced by
Honor Gould, *his twin's fiancée*! Their connection is undeniable, but
they're determined not to make the same mistake twice...

#2778 TAKING ON THE BILLIONAIRE
Redhawk Reunion • by Robin Covington
Tess Lynch once helped billionaire Adam Redhawk find his Cherokee
family. Now he needs her again—to find who's sabotaging his company.
But she has a secret agenda that doesn't stop sparks from flying. Will
the woman he can't resist be his downfall?

**YOU CAN FIND MORE INFORMATION ON UPCOMING HARLEQUIN TITLES,
FREE EXCERPTS AND MORE AT HARLEQUIN.COM.**

HDCNM11120

SPECIAL EXCERPT FROM

⬧ HARLEQUIN
DESIRE

*Looking to settle down, Alaskan CEO Garth Outlaw
thinks he wants a convenient bride. What he doesn't
know is that his pilot, Regan Fairchild, wants* him. *Now,
with two accidental weeks together in paradise, will the
wife he needs be closer than he realized?*

Read on for a sneak peek at
The Wife He Needs
by New York Times *bestselling author Brenda Jackson.*

"May I go on record to make something clear, Regan?" Garth
asked, kicking off his shoes.

She swallowed. He was standing, all six feet and three inches
of him, at the foot of the bed, staring at her with the same intensity
that she felt. She wasn't sure what he had to say, but she definitely
wanted to hear it.

"Yes," she said in an almost whisper.

"You don't need me to make you feel sexy, desired and wanted.
You are those things already. What I intend to do is to make you feel
needed," he said, stepping away from the bed to pull his T-shirt over
his head and toss it on a nearby chair. "If you only knew the depth
of my need for you."

She wondered if being needed also meant she was indispensable,
essential, vital, crucial…all those things she wanted to become to
him.

"Now I have you just where I want you, Regan. In my bed."

And whether he knew it or not, she had him just where she
wanted him, too. Standing in front of her and stripping, for starters.
As she watched, his hands went to the front of his jeans.

"And I have you doing what I've always fantasized about, Garth.
Taking your clothes off in front of me so I can see you naked."

She could tell from the look on his face that her words surprised
him. "You used to fantasize about me?"

"All the time. You always looked sexy in your business suits, but my imagination gets a little more risqué than that."

He shook his head. "I never knew."

"What? That I wanted you as much as you wanted me? I told you that in the kitchen earlier."

"I assumed that desire began since you've been here with me."

Boy, was he wrong. "No, it goes back further than that."

It was important that he knew everything. Not only that the desire was mutual but also that it hadn't just begun. If he understood that then it would be easier for her to build the kind of relationship they needed, regardless of whether he thought they needed it or not.

"I never knew," he said, looking a little confused. "You never said anything."

"I wasn't supposed to. You are my boss and I am a professional."

He nodded because she knew he couldn't refute that. "How long have you felt that way?"

There was no way she would tell him that she'd had a crush on him since she was sixteen, or that he was the reason she had returned to Fairbanks after her first year in college. She had heard he was back home from the military with a broken heart, and she'd been determined to fix it. Things didn't work out quite that way. He was deep in mourning for the woman he'd lost and had built a solid wall around himself, one that even his family hadn't been able to penetrate for a long while.

"The length of time doesn't matter, Garth. All you need to know is that the desire between us is mutual. Now, are you going to finish undressing or what?"

Don't miss what happens next in...
The Wife He Needs
by Brenda Jackson, the first book in her
Westmoreland Legacy: The Outlaws series!

Available November 2020 wherever
Harlequin Desire books and ebooks are sold.

Harlequin.com

HDEXP1120

Get 4 FREE REWARDS!

We'll send you 2 FREE Books <u>plus</u> 2 FREE Mystery Gifts.

Harlequin Desire® books transport you to the world of the American elite with juicy plot twists, delicious sensuality and intriguing scandal.

FREE Value Over $20

YES! Please send me 2 FREE Harlequin Desire novels and my 2 FREE gifts (gifts are worth about $10 retail). After receiving them, if I don't wish to receive any more books, I can return the shipping statement marked "cancel." If I don't cancel, I will receive 6 brand-new novels every month and be billed just $4.55 per book in the U.S. or $5.24 per book in Canada. That's a savings of at least 13% off the cover price! It's quite a bargain! Shipping and handling is just 50¢ per book in the U.S. and $1.25 per book in Canada.* I understand that accepting the 2 free books and gifts places me under no obligation to buy anything. I can always return a shipment and cancel at any time. The free books and gifts are mine to keep no matter what I decide.

225/326 HDN GNND

Name (please print)

Address   Apt. #

City   State/Province   Zip/Postal Code

Email: Please check this box ☐ if you would like to receive newsletters and promotional emails from Harlequin Enterprises ULC and its affiliates. You can unsubscribe anytime.

Mail to the **Reader Service:**
IN U.S.A.: P.O. Box 1341, Buffalo, NY 14240-8531
IN CANADA: P.O. Box 603, Fort Erie, Ontario L2A 5X3

Want to try 2 free books from another series! Call 1-800-873-8635 or visit www.ReaderService.com.

HD20R2

Love Harlequin romance?

DISCOVER.

Be the first to find out about promotions,
news and exclusive content!

Facebook.com/HarlequinBooks

Twitter.com/HarlequinBooks

Instagram.com/HarlequinBooks

Pinterest.com/HarlequinBooks

ReaderService.com

EXPLORE.

Sign up for the Harlequin e-newsletter and
download a free book from any series at
TryHarlequin.com

CONNECT.

Join our Harlequin community to
share your thoughts and connect
with other romance readers!
Facebook.com/groups/HarlequinConnection